My

Big

Fat

Teen

CRISIS

Look out for more from Jenny Smith

Diary of a
PARENT
TRAINER

www.jennysmithonline.com
Twitter: jennysmithbooks

MY Big Fat TEEN CRISIS

Jenny Smith

SCHOLASTIC

First published in the UK in 2012 by Scholastic Children's Books
An imprint of Scholastic Ltd
Euston House, 24 Eversholt Street
London, NW1 1DB, UK
Registered office: Westfield Road, Southam, Warwickshire, CV47 0RA
SCHOLASTIC and associated logos are trademarks and/or
registered trademarks of Scholastic Inc.

ISBN 978 1 407 115955

A CIP catalogue record for this book is available
from the British Library.

Printed and bound by CPI Group (UK) Ltd, Croydon, CR0 4YY
Papers used by Scholastic Children's Books are made from wood grown in
sustainable forests.

1 3 5 7 9 10 8 6 4 2

www.scholastic.co.uk/zone
www.jennysmithonline.com

For Susan

x

Chapter One

My name's Sam Wallis, I'm thirteen, and my life is officially over. I'm not exaggerating.

You see, my best friend in the world, Gemma, has just moved a gazillion billion miles away, and without her I honestly don't know what to do with myself.

Me and Gems used to do everything together. One of our favourite things was to do Positives and Negatives lists about stuff. I don't remember how it started, but we would do these lists about anything and everything – from the best and worst things about school trips to the advantages and disadvantages of crisp sandwiches. We'd often end up lying on the floor, our stomachs hurting from laughing so hard.

Well, now I've done one about Gemma leaving.

POSITIVES
* NONe whatsoever.

NEGATIVES

⊛ My life will never be the same.

⊛ Nobody else finds goats funny.

Since we met in primary school, Gemma and I have been inseparable. Until now, that is. We went to school together. We helped out at the local stables together. We messed about being spectacularly stupid together. If we weren't actually together we were messaging each other. It was always us against the world.

Then her parents ruined everything just before the Easter holidays by taking Gems to the Outer Hebrides. (Which, for the geographically challenged like me, are remote islands so far north of Scotland it's like they're at the North Pole or something.) This is just about the worst thing they could have done, apart from actually murdering her.

I can't believe they've taken her away, especially right in the middle of the school year.

I thought I'd be OK, but now, on the first day back, I realize that without her, I'm lost. I'm not sure if I even know who I *am* any more.

So, this morning in history, I wrote a Positives and Negatives list about myself.

POSITIVES

⊛ Longish legs.

- Blonde hair, which looks good in summer when I've got a bit of a tan.
- Hazel-coloured eyes which people say are an interesting colour.
- Good teeth... (possibly my best feature?)
- Friendly personality.
- Will laugh at anything.

NEGATIVES

- Immature (according to Tania Hamilton, who is really popular and knows about this stuff).
- Giant hands.
- Almost flat chest.
- Hair a nightmare to manage due to being so flyaway.
- Hideous nose freckles in summer.
- Blush a lot.
- Will laugh at anything - and often can't stop.
- Occasional wind problem.

Tania Hamilton says I'm immature because I've not had a proper boyfriend and because I laugh uncontrollably at things.

I suppose she has a point about the laughing. Once I start laughing, I find it hard to stop. It's like when you

3

have a coughing fit, except with me it's a sort of chortling fit. I once giggled all the way through maths, for almost an hour, because Mr Porter was wearing his cardigan inside out.

Another time I wept with laughter throughout most of a biology lesson. You see, when Mrs Nicolson put up a picture of two frogs mating, Gemma pointed out that one of them looked like our PE teacher, Mr McAllister. I was so out of control, I got sent out of the lab and had to laugh in the corridor instead.

The biology lesson incident led to me and Gemma snorting and sniggering all the way through the next few PE lessons, because every time we looked at Mr McAllister we remembered the picture of the frogs.

Maybe I *am* a slow developer. Which could explain why, while I supposedly had boyfriends when I was in Year 7, I've never actually kissed anybody. And neither has Gemma. We've been so busy mucking about and seeing the funny side of things, we're about a million miles behind everybody else when it comes to the boys thing. It's actually getting embarrassing now.

So from today onwards, I've decided that I have to make an effort to be more mature. And now that I don't have Gems around to talk things through with, I'm going to have to work it out by myself.

To make the first day back at school even worse, my history teacher, Mr Donovan (known as "Mad Eyes" Donovan due to his mad, staring eyes) was telling us all about the horrors of medieval torture. He was going into great detail. Put it this way, I was glad I'd not had scrambled eggs for breakfast.

Today, for the first time, Gemma's seat next to me did not have Gemma in it. There was a new boy sitting there instead. I didn't pay him much attention. Instead I scribbled my Positives and Negatives list on a piece of paper torn out of my homework book.

"*Samantha Wallis!*" barked Mr Donovan in his angry-sarcastic voice, his scary eyes drilling into me. "I hope that you are taking notes about the lesson. I hope that you are *not* writing something irrelevant, like last time. What was it again? Oh yes, 'My twenty favourite things to do at the weekend'. That was *very* entertaining for the class. We particularly enjoyed 'Dressing my cat as a gangster'."

Yes, I do occasionally put my cat, Scuzzball, in his Al Capone outfit, which he got for Christmas. And yes, there may be other outfits for other occasions. It's not animal cruelty. It's very entertaining.

"I'm writing about medieval torture, Mr Donovan," I lied.

"I sincerely hope you are," he said, in a menacing and threatening way. Mr Donovan is extremely good at being threatening, due to his psycho eyes. In fact, he'd have been the ideal medieval torturer, because he'd have loved his job. He'd probably have done it for free *and* put in lots of overtime.

But because you don't get "Chief Medieval Torturer"

jobs any more, Mr Donovan makes do with torturing us instead.

As a precautionary measure, I folded my Positives and Negatives list up as small as possible and hid it up my sleeve.

As I did this, I sensed the new boy at Gemma's desk watching me, and for the first time I actually looked at him. The first thing I noticed was his very blue eyes sparkling with amusement, as if he thought me dressing Scuzzball as a gangster was the most entertaining thing ever.

He had shortish, dark blond hair and a friendly face. He was smiling . . . at *me*. To my complete horror, I felt myself blush. I bowed my head as low as I could in the hope he wouldn't notice.

I've had crushes on boys before, but this was so . . . sudden. I felt as if it was so obvious . . . everyone in the room would have to notice my huge blushing reaction. This, of course, just made me blush even more. The more I blushed, the worse it got. I couldn't believe how I was reacting. It took me completely by surprise.

Sam Wallis
Still missing you enormously and immensely etc etc. I know it's only the first day back, but it's not the same without you. The corridors are too quiet without the sound of your unique squawking laugh ... which I hope is now scaring off all the seals in the Outer Hebrides. Maybe if your dad's very strange and totally

unnecessary wildlife research is ruined you can come back. Ha! That would be excellent! How are the sheep, by the way? Still munching that grass? Have you bought a kilt yet? Och aye the noo!

I am sneakily writing this in the last lesson before lunch, which is I.T. Because I finished my work early I've been allowed ten minutes to do what I want. So I thought I'd message you.

Listen. Something HUGE has happened. There's this new boy. He walked into history this morning. His name's David Matthieson.

He smiled at me, Gems, and he had such a great smile!

At the end of the lesson, he came over to me and said: "You're Sam, aren't you?" as if he already knew me! It made me feel like I was the only person in the world. I didn't know what to say. I just stammered "Yeah" and ran out of the classroom!

I think this might be it. I think I could actually be ready to have a proper boyfriend!!!! The only trouble is, why would he look at me? Tania says I look ten, and I think she's right. But then again, he did smile at me in a way that made me think I might have a chance. Please reply as soon as you can. This is an emergency.

After my message to Gems, I went into the lunch hall and sat on my own, missing her. I so needed to talk to her, and she wasn't there. I thought about the positives and negatives of having a gigantic crush on someone I'd only just met and hadn't even had a proper conversation with.

POSITIVES

* Something more interesting than the lesson to concentrate on.
* Somebody to imagine in my "Dream Wedding" fantasy.
* A reason to try to control my occasional wind problem.

NEGATIVES

* According to Tania Hamilton, I look about ten years old.
* I dress like someone who spends their weekend mucking out stables, because I do.
* Who wants to go out with someone who can't concentrate or think clearly or speak properly because they are so overcome by your amazing blue eyes?

"Hello, Little Miss No Mates!"

I looked up. It was Tania Hamilton. The last person I wanted to see when I was feeling down. It's typical of Tania to say the thing that you hope no one is thinking. She just somehow knows. Sometimes I think she likes seeing people upset.

Tania's super-confident, curvy in all the right places (unlike me), great at netball and good-looking, even if she does wear most of the make-up counter at Boots. She even manages to make our school uniform look vaguely fashionable, which is a major achievement, believe me.

There was no way I was going to answer back. Nobody wants to take Tania on; she's far too capable of shaming you in front of the whole lunch hall. Most of the boys fancy her, and some of the girls secretly wish they could be as outspoken as her – but *everybody* is wary of her.

Because nobody stands up to her, Tania carries on randomly picking on people and thinking that it's a great joke. Occasionally she is actually funny, annoyingly. Last year on non-uniform day, for example, she came in dressed as Miss Mooney. I have to admit, it was hilarious. In fact, I think I laughed for most of the day.

"Hello," I said, taking the safe option. I thought for one horrible moment that she was going to sit down, but to my relief she walked on and joined her two regular lunch buddies, Angela Murray and Becky Robinson. Angela is Tania's sidekick. She always laughs when Tania's mean.

I dislike Angela even more than I dislike Tania because at least Tania's got her own mind. Angela just follows whatever Tania does, like a sheep. In fact, Angela even looks slightly like a sheep.

I think Becky would rather not be in Tania's little gang, but she's scared to leave because Tania might murder her or, worse, say horrible things about her. So she just goes along with things.

Angela and Becky are on the netball team with Tania, which is how they've got to be friends. Tania didn't bother asking if I'd like to join them, not that I'd have wanted to. She smirked at me as she sat down, then whispered something to Angela, who looked at me and laughed loudly.

I did what I always do when Tania is mean. I imagined her being chased by a goat. Me and Gems thought that one up: we've always found goats funny. So I imagined Tania, screaming in terror, running across the lunch hall with a big angry goat after her. I'd advise anyone to use what we call The Goat Scenario in such situations. It's very effective.

Darcie Clelland, my lab partner from chemistry, was sitting with her best friend, Hanna Kermack, at the other end of the lunch hall. Darcie's very straightforward and matter-of-fact, but with a quiet sense of humour. Hanna was at primary with me and Gemma, and is really good-natured and dependable. Me and Gems often had lunch with them.

They waved across at me, motioning for me to join them. I was just about to get up when I saw the last person in the world I expected to see, standing uncertainly in the middle of the lunch hall, holding a tray.

Catrina Malloy. Or Cat, as she's always been called.

I could hardly believe it.

Although I'd not seen her for six years, it was obviously

Cat. She was looking around as if hoping to find a familiar face. I waved, and when she saw me her face lit up.

From when I was tiny until I was seven, Cat was my best friend. Our mums met at the mother and baby group, and because they were friends, we were friends. I suppose you don't have much choice about who you hang out with if you're in nappies and unable to walk. Your mums decide, and that's that.

My very first memory is of being in a sandpit with Cat, fighting over a shiny red plastic beaker. She won, but I don't remember being upset about it. There are other memories, of sunlit back gardens, and ice cream, and running around in Snow White and Cinderella costumes, and sharing a beanbag, watching the Teletubbies. I liked La La the best; Cat preferred Dipsy.

I remember our mums and dads having dinner together. Me and Cat would play long elaborate games with hundreds of dolls and cuddly toys while they drank wine and laughed, and one of us would be carried home, which was only round the corner.

Another memory. The school nativity. Cat sang "Twinkle, Twinkle, Little Star" so beautifully, all the mums were crying.

When I was about seven, Cat disappeared from my life. I vaguely remember that our mums drifted apart. Cat never came back to school after the summer holidays.

Then, three years later, out of the blue, I got a postcard. It was from Cornwall. I didn't know if she lived there, or if she was on holiday. It said, in her neat and careful rounded handwriting, that she missed me, but there was no home address on it, so I couldn't reply. She never wrote again.

The girl now walking across the lunch hall towards me was stunning. She had the same flawless olive skin and long, thick glossy black hair that I remembered. Cat doesn't look anything like her petite, blonde mother; her looks come entirely from her father.

There was a loud wolf whistle. Cat ignored it, although it was clearly directed at her. And no wonder. I couldn't stop staring at her. She looked like a model. Her almond-shaped brown eyes were accentuated with black eyeliner, and her hair was swept up into an effortless ponytail. A short black skirt showed off her impossibly long slim legs. She was wearing non-regulation purple nail varnish. Everybody in the lunch hall was turning to look at her.

Tania Hamilton was no longer smiling. In fact she looked almost angry at the attention Cat was getting.

"Hello," Cat said, grinning, plonking her tray down and sitting opposite me, seemingly oblivious to the stir she'd caused. I sat looking at her, still shocked. I'd thought I'd never see her again.

"What are you doing here?" I managed at last.

"Well, thanks for the enthusiastic welcome," Cat said, still smiling.

I smiled back.

"It is so good to see you," I said. I meant it.

"Good to see you too," said Cat. "And you haven't

changed one bit! I can't believe I'm here. This is so weird."

"Where were you?" I asked, expecting her to say Cornwall or Spain or something like that. After all, she'd seemingly disappeared from the face of the earth.

"We were in Bredborough," she said.

Bredborough is the nearest big town to Greenfields. It's close enough that people can commute there for work. It's not a million miles away, but it might as well be if you don't know where to find somebody.

I couldn't believe it. All that time and she'd only been in Bredborough. Now it seemed even more strange that our mums hadn't got back in touch with each other.

"Bredborough?" I couldn't hide my surprise.

Cat looked down, finding it difficult to meet my gaze.

"Lots happened. That's why Mum never got back in touch. She wasn't . . . well," she said. "Then Dad left."

"Your mum wasn't well?" I echoed. I didn't remember her mum being ill.

She looked up and met my questioning look. I could see she was struggling with whether to say something. Eventually she decided to speak, and leant forward.

"Mum was really messed up," she whispered, "but she's OK now."

"So you're back in Greenfields," I managed, after a long pause. There's nothing like stating the obvious to fill a silence.

"Yes," said Cat. "Gran died just before Christmas, so we moved back because Mum inherited the house."

"Oh, sorry," I said. So her gran had died, as well as her mum and dad splitting up. It made me realize what an easy time I've had in comparison. Maybe my life wasn't so bad after all.

We sat in silence for a little while. Then Cat spoke again.

"Things are OK now, really. I mean, Mum and Dad are talking again, and Mum's sorted herself out. She's painting."

I remembered that Cat's mum was a painter. It was all coming back to me now. I still couldn't believe that Cat was sitting opposite me. After all those years.

"So, what are you doing now?" I asked.

"Not much," said Cat, "except I've just joined this band, you might have heard of them. They're called Mr Bleaney."

"*Mr Bleaney?*" I gasped, stunned.

Mr Bleaney are this band people are starting to talk about. They go to the upper school and are all about sixteen or seventeen. I first saw them last summer, at the Greenfields town festival.

"The singer left," explained Cat. "Someone from my last school told me about it, so I tried out and they chose me. I still can't believe it."

I looked at Cat, who's six months older than me, and thought how much older than thirteen she looks. She could easily pass for sixteen. With her looks and her singing voice, which was good even when she was tiny, it was no wonder the band wanted her.

14

"That's so great!" I burst out, delighted. This, at least, was something to be happy about.

Cat smiled, pleased that I was pleased for her.

Some boys at the next table were clowning around. I knew it was to try to get Cat's attention, because they kept looking over to see if she was noticing them. She wasn't.

I noticed that, just like Tania, Cat seemed to have the knack of transforming our school uniform into something that looked good. I never seem to quite manage it. I think I'm too scruffy. My school shirt's always coming untucked and my jumper's covered in little bobbles from Scuzzball's claws. But I do try with my hair, at least.

"It's fantastic to see you again," said Cat, her eyes shining. It was exactly the way she smiled when we were little, as if she were lit up from the inside. This was the Cat I remembered. Suddenly it was as if the six years we'd been apart never existed and we were starting again where we'd left off.

Tania Hamilton was looking across, practically seething with jealousy. She was not appreciating the way the boys were putting on a show for Cat.

"Why were you sitting on your own?" asked Cat.

I could tell she was puzzled.

"My best friend . . . Gemma . . . left," I said. "Her parents took her to the Outer Hebrides. She's not happy about it."

"That's how it works," said Cat, looking sorry. I didn't know what to say. I'm not good at sad stuff. There was another silence.

I had just decided to cheer Cat up by telling her some funny stories about Gemma when we were rudely interrupted.

"Fair maidens . . . mayest your humble servant dine with thee?"

I looked up. It was Taylor Griffen, of all people. He was obviously desperate to check out the new girl. He's been speaking in that stupid Ye Olde English way ever since he heard we were going to study *Romeo and Juliet* this term.

Taylor's one of these people it's impossible to ignore. While he's on the small side, his personality is enormous. He has this round face, round blue eyes and corkscrew-curly blond hair so he looks quite angelic, but he's far from it. He's a mischief-maker extraordinaire. He's like an attention-seeking missile, working his way around Year 8 causing hilarity and mayhem, flirting outrageously with all the girls.

Everybody loves Taylor – even Tania can't help being amused by him. But he can be quite tiring to be around, because he's constantly making some sort of a scene.

"Verily, Sam, prithee present us to thy most fair companion!" boomed Taylor. For someone who is smallish, he's got a very loud voice. People around us were sniggering at Taylor's over-the-top display. Taylor was oblivious. It's like he's got a rhinoceros hide instead of skin.

I couldn't believe he was making even more of an idiot of himself than normal, thinking it would impress Cat.

"This is Cat. Cat, this is Taylor," I said.

Taylor's round eyes widened with the shock of recognition.

"Catrina *Malloy*? It's you! We were at primary school together! Do you remember me?"

"Taylor, we're just having a bit of a catch up, it's not really a good time. . ." I said, hoping he'd take the hint.

"Of course I remember you," said Cat. She smiled again, showing her perfect white teeth. "You're not someone it's easy to forget!"

She was right. Even at primary, Taylor was a force to be reckoned with. I remembered him trying to kiss all the girls, even then. And come to think of it, he'd followed Cat around for quite a long time in Year 3.

This was just like Cat, I remembered, to be kind even to the most annoying people. She never liked to see anybody excluded. Even at nursery school she would go out of her way to make sure nobody was left out.

I wondered if she understood the danger of being kind to Taylor Griffen.

I could see he was spellbound. He dropped to one knee and kissed her hand, as if he were Sir Lancelot. As I might have guessed, one smile from the beautiful Cat, and he was instantly her slave.

In chemistry, Darcie did everything while I idled. I stared into the flame of the Bunsen burner.

"What's *wrong* with you?" she asked at one point. I'm usually quite keen in chemistry, as I secretly hope that I might

17

accidentally make some major breakthrough scientific discovery. Like something that will reverse the ageing process, or make you invisible, or give you the power of flight.

"Life," I said, "can be just *so strange*."

"Nonsense," said Darcie, in her usual matter-of-fact way, "it all makes perfect sense. Everything's governed by cause and effect."

I thought about her cause and effect theory and tried to apply it to my immediate situation.

Cause: First day back at school without Gemma.

Effect: Major crisis.

Cause: Gorgeous new boy in history gives me amazing smile.

Effect: My first major crush.

Cause: Cat turning up at school after my not seeing her for six years.

Effect: Surprised and pleased.

No wonder I was feeling confused. This was quite a lot for one morning.

MY STATUS
Sam Wallis
Is missing Gemma loads.
Gemma Smith likes this.

Chapter Two

Greenfields is a big market town about an hour from London.

I live in a modern, red-brick semi-detached house in a cul-de-sac on the outskirts. I have to share it with Mum, Dad and my older brother Ryan. And of course Scuzzball, the best-dressed cat in Greenfields.

We're a very ordinary family living in a pretty ordinary house in an ordinary sort of town. Even my parents do ordinary jobs. Mum's a nurse at the local health centre. Dad's the local butcher.

Having a dad who is a butcher definitely has its positives and negatives.

POSITIVES

* I will never die of protein deficiency or anaemia.
* I will not starve or have my growth stunted by malnutrition.

NEGATIVES

- Dinner is always meat and two veg. ALWAYS. Never, ever pasta and lasagne and pizza like other people have.
- Dad smells of raw meat.
- If I ever by some miracle get a proper boyfriend before I'm thirty, Dad will frighten him off with his collection of giant meat cleavers and terrifying bone-breaking implements.

I got home from school to find that Mum was in a bad mood. She was just home from work, still wearing her nurse's uniform. She's been forced to do lots of extra shifts recently, and it's been taking its toll on her. Then she comes home and Dad and Ryan don't help round the house. No wonder she gets stressed out so easily these days.

"The house is *falling apart*," she moaned, pointing to the kitchen door handle, which had come off yet again. Dad keeps pretending to mend it, but doesn't have a clue about what he's doing. Mum's right about the house, it *is* falling apart. It hasn't been decorated for years.

"Your Auntie Penny's house is like the ones in the *Ideal Home* magazine," said Mum, wistfully. "She keeps emailing me pictures of her new kitchen."

Auntie Penny is my mum's sister who lives in Australia. When she's not emailing Mum pictures of her new kitchen, she's constantly commenting on my status on Facebook since I stupidly and thoughtlessly accepted her friend request a year ago, when I was still young and naive. Gemma was equally stupid and friended her too, so we are both cursed with Auntie Penny's cringe-making remarks. She says things like "did you enjoy your disco-party?" and she thinks LOL means "lots of love" which means she'll say things like "Sorry you had such a bad day. LOL."

I wish she'd stop. People her age shouldn't be on Facebook. They should have their own social network called Prehistoricbook.

"Where's Ryan?" I asked, hoping to distract Mum from her kitchen envy.

Ryan's sixteen and completely toadlike. He specializes in emptying the fridge and cupboards of all food, hiding in his room, and playing guitar for hours with his equally toadlike friend Matthew.

"He's in his room," Mum said, "Matthew's round. Your dad's bringing home some pork for dinner. By the way, do you know what day it is today?"

"No," I said. I racked my brains. It was nobody's birthday.

"It's our anniversary, me and your dad's. Not just any anniversary, either. It's our *twentieth* anniversary. And do you know what? Not even a card!"

She was emptying the dishwasher. When she got to the cutlery she started practically flinging it into the drawer. Scuzzball flew out of the kitchen in alarm like a guided missile. He's an extremely jumpy cat. I can't think why. He has a nice life, and a wardrobe most cats would kill for.

"Maybe he's got something planned for later," I said, in my optimistic way. Although if I were to be realistic, I'd have to admit that Dad's not the type to remember anniversaries. He's far more concerned about prime ribs.

I took advantage of Mum's disbelieving silence to tell her about Cat.

"So they've moved back to Greenfields, just Catrina and her mother?" she said, looking genuinely surprised.

"Yes, they're living at her gran's house. She left it to Cat's mum."

"I see," said Mum, thoughtfully. "Maybe I should get in touch with Eileen again. I'd love to catch up with her."

I went up to my room and lay on the bed with my laptop, hoping that Gemma had messaged me back. Of course she had. She doesn't have much else to do up in the Outer Hebrides, after all.

Gemma Smith
OMG!!!!!!!!!! You have GOT TO FIND OUT MORE ABOUT HIM. I want lots of information.
In case our messages get intercepted by enemy agents, you must call him LOML. I will call him LOYL as he is not – obviously – the love of my life (seeing as I've never met him).

This is so exciting. You must message me constantly, especially since I can't get a good enough signal on my phone for us to talk.

My life is as boring as I dreaded it would be here. Dad goes out and looks at seals. Mum's writing her book about the history of the milk churn. WHY did I get the bonkers parents? There are only twelve of us in the whole school here!! Only two other teenagers, both girls, and I've just found out their main hobby is knitting. There is nobody cute within a hundred miles. I should just throw myself into the sea.

Have not bought kilt yet. Might as well. There's nobody here to impress.

Do you think he likes you back? What did your hair look like?

Gemma knows me so well. She knows how important it is to me that my hair looks OK. My hair can be hideously flyaway. It's a constant trauma.

Sometimes my hair behaves itself and looks good, and sometimes it doesn't and I look like I've been given an electric shock. Luckily, as I've said, today it was on its best behaviour. I explained this to Gems when I finally got her on chat.

Sam Wallis
Hair looked <u>fab</u>. I am a goddess. Will find out more and let you know. Don't throw yourself into the sea. Throw your mum and dad in instead. It's their fault, after all.

Enjoy that you're under no pressure to look good. Get one of those tartan hats with the red wig attached.

Gemma Smith
Might as well get tartan wig-hat. My life is officially over. Look out of the window and just see sheep. Help! What else is new?

Sam Wallis
Remember Catrina Malloy, my friend when I was little? She's turned up at Grungefields! She had lunch with me today cos she doesn't know anyone. It was so weird to see her again.

Gemma Smith
OMG!!! Yes, I remember her from Greenfields Primary. Very pretty, with dark hair? She disappeared off somewhere and you were like a lost soul without her. I had to rescue you.

Sam Wallis
She looks about sixteen now, so I look tres immature in comparison. The boys were all staring at her cos she's so good-looking. Girls all v. jealous of her. Tania Hamilton looked really annoyed!!

Gemma Smith
So you are replacing me with a new BF? I KNEW IT!

Sam Wallis

How could anyone replace you? Anyway, it was you who replaced her, remember? She's lovely, but Cat would never understand ironic sweatshirt wearing, and she would never in a million years get why we find goats funny. Actually, why DO we find goats funny? When did <u>that</u> start?

Gemma Smith

Glad she doesn't understand about goats. It started in the last year of primary, when we went on that outing to the farm and Mrs Prentiss got attacked by an evil-looking goat and everyone but us was crying and screaming, and we were laughing. Don't you remember? It tore a hole in her skirt. You laughed all the way home on the bus.

Mum and I were sitting in the kitchen later when Dad burst in. I had brought my laptop down to do my homework at the kitchen table, while Mum was doing a crossword puzzle and listening to the radio. Dad looked spectacularly pleased with himself.

Dad is not short, but not tall. He's sort of compact, muscular, and hairy. That makes him sound like a dwarf from *The Lord of the Rings*, which is not what he looks like. He's got a round, red, cheery sort of a face, dark hair and thick black eyebrows, and no matter how often he shaves he always seems to have stubble on his chin. He's all-right-looking, I suppose, but not as attractive as Mum.

"Happy anniversary!" he bellowed, holding up a plastic bag as if it was a trophy. "I've got your present."

My heart sank when I saw the bag. It was one of the red-striped ones from his shop. I could see the telltale blood which had leaked from the paper package inside it.

Dad continued to wave the bag as if he'd brought Mum a priceless diamond necklace.

"Forget pork! I only said that to put you off the scent. To celebrate our twenty years together I've brought us back the *best rib-eye steak you'll have ever tasted*."

Mum continued with the crossword as if she'd not heard him. Dad didn't pick up on her complete lack of enthusiasm. He's too thick-skinned. He rubbed his hands together briskly.

"We're going to have the meal of our lives!"

Mum looked up and said, "Six across. Twelve letters. First letter *d*, third letter *s*. 'To fail to have one's expectation fulfilled in some regard'."

Then she went upstairs.

"Mmmm, twelve letters. No, I can't get it," said Dad, totally oblivious as usual.

"Disappointed," I said.

"What?"

"That's the answer to the crossword clue: *disappointed*."

"Oh," said Dad, still not getting it. There was no such clue. I checked afterwards.

Mum came back down wearing a dress that quite suits her, but that she's had for years. She got on with preparing the vegetables. Dad, of course, did not notice she'd changed. He was too busy talking about the steaks and telling us how the cows were reared on organic watercress or something. Sometimes I think he doesn't notice much at all. He never sees that he's upset Mum. He assumes everybody is constantly upbeat like him.

Ryan and Matthew appeared, like vampires startled by daylight. Possessed by the curse of teenage freakdom and general hormonal turmoil, they were both covered in giant boil-type spots. No wonder they're always playing mournful songs on the guitar together. It must be pretty depressing to be so toadlike.

After Matthew shuffled out, mumbling something that might have been "goodbye", Dad insisted that we set the table specially and light some candles. He opened a bottle of our best wine, one we'd got for Christmas. It was covered in dust – not because it was vintage wine, but because our house is dusty.

I changed Scuzzball into his dinner-jacket outfit, complete with miniature pink bow tie, so we could take a photograph of him with Mum and Dad. While Scuzzball looked frankly fed up, the exercise seemed to cheer Mum up a little. I sincerely hope that if I ever make it to twenty years of marriage I get a better present than a hunk of rib-eye steak.

Despite the horrendous present, Mum tried to get into the spirit of things with their anniversary. She's far too nice. So when Dad leant across the table to give her a giant smooch, she didn't object. In fact, she smooched back.

Horrified, Ryan bolted to his room. Equally disgusted by their behaviour, I decided to go for a run. It seemed the safest course of action in case things escalated and became hideous and trauma-inducing.

Sam Wallis
I have officially turned into a STALKER! Love has made me crazy.

Gemma Smith
LOL. Tell me more.

Sam Wallis
It happened by accident. Went out after dinner for a run to get away from unexpected and very wrong snogging incident between Mum and Dad.
Anyway, was about to turn into our street on way home when saw David Matthieson, or LOML as you want me to call him, turn into it ahead of me. Followed him at a safe distance.

Gemma Smith
Definitely stalking behaviour. Wot happened next??????

Sam Wallis
You WOULD NOT believe this but guess what? He only went into the house FIVE DOORS DOWN from us!!! The one that had the "To Let" sign up for ages. I am in total

shock. I've not seen him when I've been walking home from school this week so can only assume he does something after school and comes home later!

Gemma Smith
See anything else?

Sam Wallis
Lurked outside his house for a minute, peering round hedge. Then the side door opened. I thought it was him so jumped back behind large recycling bin. Wasn't him; was his mum!!!!

Gemma Smith
Wot's she like? Scary?

Sam Wallis
No. She was taking out the dustbin. Longish brown hair in a ponytail and faded jeans and a T-shirt. She's quite old, at least forty. Had to leave at this point as she was heading straight for recycling bin.

Gemma Smith
You are rubbish stalker ha ha.

Sam Wallis
Maybe, but have found out some truly shocking information about LOML and his family.

Gemma Smith

Go on then.

Sam Wallis

Got home to find Mum loading dishwasher, while Dad was watching TV and Ryan was still hiding in his room. Asked Mum if she knew about the new people in the street. Well, she does. Guess who she heard it from.

Gemma Smith

Nosy Norah?

Sam Wallis

You got it. Nosy Norah next door told Mum that the dad is nowhere to be seen, so she thinks they are divorced. She says there's a teenage boy (obviously LOML) and a little girl called Jessica who's about six or seven. The mum's an acupuncturist.

Gemma Smith

Wot's an acupuncturist?

Sam Wallis

One of those experts who sticks pins in people. Don't you know anything, you dimwit?

Gemma Smith

Pins? Ouch. I wouldn't like that. But I don't think that it's truly shocking news, that LOYL's mum sticks pins in people.

Sam Wallis

That's not the shocking news. This is. According to Nosy Norah, they get the *Vegetarian Times* delivered, and when I was hiding by the recycling bin I saw an empty packet sticking out labelled "Marinated Tofu Pieces"!

Gemma Smith

!!!!!!!!!!!!!!!!!!!!!!!!!! Hahahahahahahahahahaha. They are vegetarians and your dad's a butcher!!!!!!!

Sam Wallis

It's NOT FUNNY.

Gemma Smith

Is too.

Sam Wallis

Not talking to you. Goodnight.

Gemma Smith

Too funny.

Sam Wallis

I have a cursed life. WHY ME?

MY STATUS
Sam Wallis

Is shocked to find that her parents have been married to each other for TWENTY YEARS. You get a shorter sentence when you commit murder.

Darcie Clelland and **Gemma Smith** like this.

Penny Griffiths I remember it was such a lovely day! Please wish your mum and dad a very happy anniversary.

Chapter Three

This morning I made a cheese and tomato sandwich for my lunch instead of my usual ham. I do *not* want David Matthieson to come into the lunch hall to see me chomping down on a piece of piggy-wig, do I? Just in case he's interested in me, I don't want to blow it. So I'm going to have to become a vegetarian during school hours to be on the safe side.

It can be hard when you like someone and you're not sure if they like you back.

POSITIVES

* I still have hope.

NEGATIVES

* I might be delusional.
* My life is confusing enough already.

I was disappointed when David wasn't in any of my classes in the morning. He'd seemed so friendly in history, more than he needed to be, I decided. And he'd remembered my name, and come up to me at the end of the lesson. So there was definitely some hope.

Cat came and sat with me again at lunch time. I still couldn't get over seeing her again, it was so strange, but it was also as if we'd slipped straight back into our old friendship. There was lots to catch up on.

During the course of the conversation I told her about Ryan hiding in his room because of teenage freakdom, and grunting rather than talking. About Mum being fed up due to Dad being more interested in rib-eye steak than romance. And about my crush on the possibly vegetarian new boy in history. I wanted to know if she thought I was mad, pretending to be a veggie nutkin myself.

"You need to find out if he likes you," said Cat thoughtfully as she picked at her salad, "or if he's just being friendly because he's that sort of person."

"Shh!" I hissed. I dreaded David Matthieson coming up behind us while we discussed how much I liked him. Not that he was in the lunch hall or anywhere to be seen. I'd checked. If you measure a crush on a scale of one to ten, this was closer to the ten than the one. I mean, you must like someone a lot if you are looking for them everywhere and prepared to give up ham.

"So, what are you going to do?" Cat looked interested.

"I don't know. I'd like to find out more about him. I already know he lives in my street. That's a start."

"What's his name?" Suddenly Cat looked as if she might know who I was talking about.

"David Matthieson," I told her, and Cat grinned broadly, looking delighted.

"Do you know him?" I asked.

"Yes," she said "Really well! He went to Bredborough Secondary too; he was in some of my classes. David's great. He's really . . . *decent*. I should have thought it might be him. I mean, I knew he was coming here and I know his family's vegetarian, but I didn't put two and two together. It's so funny that you like him!"

So Cat knew David Matthieson! This was a surprise. I wondered if I liked it, that he was friends with someone as ridiculously good-looking as Cat.

"Look! Taylor's coming, let's change the subject," I said, "but you mustn't tell anyone about this or I'll have to kill you. And you can't tell David Matthieson that my dad's a butcher."

"I won't say a word," she said.

I decided to interrogate her properly later.

Taylor sat down with an overexaggerated sigh.

"What's wrong?" I asked.

"Poor Sir Griffen is in terrible danger! Mistress Tania hath forbidden me from speaking with thee," said Taylor. "My very life may be in peril!"

"Then why are you here?" I couldn't help smiling; Taylor was looking so tragic and melodramatic.

35

"Fair maidens, how could I restraineth myself?" he said. "I am spellbound by your charms! Anyway, why should I do what Tania says? We're the old gang from Greenfields Primary, aren't we?"

I couldn't believe that Tania had tried to get him not to talk to us. It was unbelievable. I looked over and saw her glaring at Taylor, and wondered if his life really might be in danger. Certainly Tania was taller than him, and probably stronger. I imagined them in some sort of unarmed combat, fighting to the death.

During the rest of lunch, as Taylor entertained us with very funny impressions of different members of staff, I noticed that quite a few boys were still staring at Cat longingly from across the lunch hall, as if she was the first girl they'd ever seen. I wondered, for a brief but uncomfortable moment, if David Matthieson had ever looked at Cat that way.

When I walked into my English class in the afternoon, he was there, just as I'd been hoping.

This time he wasn't sitting beside me; he was three rows behind. I didn't like that because I wanted to be able to look at him without it being too obvious. This way, I'd have to spin my head round like someone possessed by Satan. Not an attractive look.

We were reading Shakespeare's *Romeo and Juliet*. Taught by Miss Mooney. All teachers have habits, and Miss Mooney's are: 1) eating loads of Polo mints and 2) saying

"Use your *imagination*!" (Which is much better than our physics teacher Mr Ashcroft's habits, which are 1) scratching his knees, 2) talking with his eyes shut and 3) saying "Work through the problem!")

Miss Mooney was in a good mood, because she's recently got engaged to the knee-scratching Mr Ashcroft and is about to change her name. She thinks that this will stop us calling her Loony Mooney behind her back. It won't.

Anyway, Miss Mooney was all happy and enthusiastic, using her imagination about her future with Mr Ashcroft. Which is the worst possible mood for a teacher to be in, when faced with our class. They can only be disappointed.

"Get out your books!" she trilled. "Has everybody got their books? Here, you can have an extra copy. Now settle down! We're going to read from page forty-three. Samantha! You can be Juliet. Taylor, you can be Romeo."

Taylor's mum's been sending him to performing arts classes since he was five. This is probably why he's so ridiculously confident. He fully expects a career on the West End stage, and then Broadway. He asked Miss Mooney if he could stand up because it helps him to project his already loud and booming voice.

"What a good idea, Taylor," she said. "Sam, why don't you stand up too?"

I stood up, clutching my book, avoiding looking at anyone, especially David Matthieson.

Taylor launched into his speech, clutching at his heart

as he boomed: "'But soft! What light through yonder window breaks? It is the east, and Juliet is the sun. . .'"

It was quite a long speech, with him gushing on about me being as fair as stars in heaven and all that. Then I had to say "Aye, me!" and then we had to go on about names or something. The worst bit was when we had to swear our undying love for each other. While I muttered my lines with no enthusiasm whatsoever, Taylor threw himself into the part with abandon. He was so over the top, people were falling about laughing.

There was a bit where he said, "Oh, wilt thou leave me so unsatisfied?" and I had to say, "What satisfaction canst thou have tonight?" when Tania Hamilton shouted, "Romeo's up for it!" which made everyone laugh even more.

When it was over, I thought my humiliation was complete. But it wasn't. At the end of the class, David Matthieson came up to me.

"You dropped this yesterday," he said.

He handed me a folded-up sheet of paper, and my heart sank when I realized what it was. Yes, you've guessed it. It was the Positives and Negatives list I'd written in history about myself. The one where I talked about all my gruesome bad points.

Unable to look him in the eye, I muttered "thanks" and walked away with as much dignity as I could manage.

I didn't do much that evening, aside from curling up in a ball and rocking back and forth, hugging Sid the knitted monkey (who shares my bed) and whimpering gently.

I did find time, between traumatic flashbacks, to chat online to Gems.

> **Sam Wallis**
> Emergency. My life is officially over. Did a Positives and Negatives list about myself, but dropped it and LOML found it. It mentioned my giant hands, my lack of chest AND my occasional wind problem.

At this point there was a long pause of almost five minutes. I knew this was because Gemma was literally rolling on the floor laughing. I'd have done exactly the same in her position. At least she was sensitive enough not to do a "hahahahahahahahahaha" response.

> **Gemma Smith**
> OMG! That's really bad. Bad. Bad. Bad. Bad. Bad.

> **Sam Wallis**
> Wot can I do?????

> **Gemma Smith**
> Come to Outer Hebrides. You are right; your life is over.

The next day, at lunchtime, I was sitting with Cat when Taylor joined us again. I was still feeling traumatized, and annoyed at myself. I decided that I also had good reason to be annoyed with Taylor.

"How could you *embarrass* me like that?" I blurted out as he sat down.

"How did he embarrass you?" asked Cat.

"He made me *stand up* to read as Juliet in English. *And* David Matthieson was there."

My words trailed off as I realized my mistake. I'd managed to let slip in front of Taylor that I like David Matthieson! Why? Why? WHY could I not keep my mouth shut?

"You'd better not blab about this," I said threateningly. I can be reasonably scary when I want to be.

Taylor looked absolutely delighted. His round blue eyes shone with mischief.

"Worry ye not, Mistress Sam, your secret is safe, locked within my bosom," he said, putting his hand on his heart as if he was still Romeo. I could practically see his mind whirring as he worked out how he could use this new information to his advantage.

"It'd better be," I said.

"Verily, I could tell thee information of great interest about David Matthieson," Taylor went on. I wasn't surprised. Taylor is a worse gossip than any girl I know, which is why I was so worried.

"Go on, then, what do you know?" I asked.

"He partaketh of his lunch in the library each day," Taylor said. "Legend has it he was almost banished from Bredborough Secondary for most evil deeds."

"Did you know about this?" I turned to Cat. "What did he do?"

"He bunked off school a few times, and he got into a couple of fights," Cat said, flicking her glossy hair over her shoulder.

I was surprised. He really didn't look like the type.

"Why's he eating his lunch in the library?" I wondered.

"He's catching up on schoolwork, science and maths stuff he missed last year," Cat said.

"So why was he falling behind on his work and getting into fights at Bredborough?" I persisted. I was puzzled.

Cat shrugged, looking uncomfortable.

"Listen, he's all right," she said, "really."

I got the feeling that she wasn't keen on talking much more about the subject. There was something about David Matthieson she was holding back. She was probably being careful because of Taylor the loudmouth being there. I decided I'd ask her more when we were alone together.

MY STATUS
Sam Wallis
Hates Romeo and Juliet.
Angela Murray, Gemma Smith and 3 others like this.
Taylor Griffin I'm not going to take that personally.
Tania Hamilton I think you should, Romeo.

Chapter Four

When I got home Mum was finishing cleaning out Ryan's fish tank, because he'd left it for ages and the poor fish were clearly going to die swimming around in green goo if nobody sorted them out.

Then she lugged out a giant basket of wet washing to hang on the line. I went out to help her. After all, nobody else would.

"How long do you think she'll take today?" Mum said.

"I give her three minutes," I replied.

We were talking about our neighbour, Norah, who is very, very nosy. Which is why we call her Nosy Norah.

Norah is a one-woman neighbourhood watch. Nothing happens in our street without Norah knowing all the details.

POSITIVES

* We are highly unlikely to be burgled.

42

- If we are burgled, the burglar will be caught on that high resolution CCTV camera Nosy Norah set up.
- We get to hear about what all our other neighbours are up to, and all their terrible secrets.

NEGATIVES
- Our neighbours know what we've been up to, and all our terrible secrets.

Nosy Norah lives on her own. She's retired from her job as a school secretary and now has far too much time on her hands, so her hobby is finding out what everyone is up to. You can rely on Norah to stick her head over our fence at every opportunity to spread the latest gossip.

Sure enough, her head popped up a minute or so later. You could tell she was having to stand on tiptoe to see over the fence.

"Hope it stays dry for you," she said, by way of hello, her eyes shining with mischief, made to look enormous by the thick lenses of her glasses.

"I think we'll be all right," replied Mum, also fluent in the language of weather. "I like your hair."

Norah's grey hair was cut in a new style. She looked very pleased. Almost too pleased for it just to be about her haircut.

"I have HUGE news!" she said.

"Oh," said Mum, pegging a pair of my dad's horrible burgundy Y-fronts firmly to the line.

"I've won a competition!" said Nosy Norah, slightly breathless. "It's a *luxury Caribbean cruise for two*!"

"Norah, that's wonderful!" enthused Mum. "How did you win it?"

"To be honest," said Nosy Norah, "I'm not sure. I enter competitions all the time, so I can't remember! I got a phone call this morning, but they're sending all the details by registered post. I still can't believe it!"

"Well, let me know when I should start packing!" joked Mum.

"I will!" said Nosy Norah.

Back in the house, I peeled the potatoes while Mum unloaded the dishwasher.

"That's lucky for Norah," I remarked.

Mum sighed. "I've got a horrible feeling about it. People ring you all the time about these supposedly free cruises. Then, when you get the details, there's often a catch, like you have to pay for all your own meals on board, and it turns out to be like a glorified car ferry with tiny uncomfortable cabins where you're taken to tourist destinations and expected to part with more money. I'm afraid she might be in for a disappointment."

"Why didn't you say anything?" I asked.

"I didn't want to embarrass her," said Mum. "She'll find out soon enough and we won't say any more about it."

Mum's nice that way; she thinks about people's feelings

and goes out of her way to make people feel comfortable. I think that's the nurse part of her: she's good with people. Mum and Norah get on really well, despite being so different. Mum's been extra kind to her since her husband died a few years ago, and I think Norah appreciates it.

After dinner, I found Gems was online, so had a chat with her, which was good.

Gemma Smith
How's the mad stalker? R u going to put up a shrine to LOYL in your bedroom?

Sam Wallis
Already have, have got a giant picture of him surrounded by vegetables and soya products. Things have not improved. Had to be Juliet to Taylor Griffin's Romeo, IN FRONT OF HIM!! Have also found out he got into fights and bunked from his last school.

Gemma Smith
So he's a bad boy! I can't believe he lives in the same street as you. I can't believe he's a VEGETARIAN!!! Most of all I can't believe he saw your Positives and Negatives list. I laughed so much yesterday; Mum thought I was having a seizure. She was v. annoyed as she likes peace and quiet when she's writing. It takes a lot of concentration to write about the history of milk churns, apparently.

Sam Wallis

How are the Outer Hebrides? No sign of any boys?

Gemma Smith

Only sheep. Shoot me now. Things as boring as ever. The two girls in the school who're my age – Shona and Elaine – are trying to get me interested in knitting.

Sam Wallis

LOL. Granny alert. Do they have blue rinses and perms?

Gemma Smith

V. funny!! No, they look normal. It turns out all the knitting is a money-making scheme. They sell the stuff they make to tourist shops for loads of money. They asked me round today after school and tried to teach me! And what's worse, I quite enjoyed it!!!

Sam Wallis

No WAY. Are you ill?

Gemma Smith

It must be sheer desperation at having nothing else to do. I've decided to knit you a green hat and scarf for your birthday so I hope you appreciate it.

Sam Wallis

Really, you shouldn't. I insist.

Gemma Smith

But I must. That's how much I love you as a friend. Talking of which, how is your new BF?

Sam Wallis

Cat? She is settling in OK. Turns out she knows LOML from Bredborough Secondary, so trying to find out useful information from her. How are you going to find a boyfriend? Now you've joined this knitting circle, maybe you'll all knit giant nets and then catch boys out of the sea or something.

Gemma Smith

You may not be so far from the truth. It turns out Shona and Elaine know about some opportunities to meet boys of our age. But they're being all mysterious about what these are. Will have to keep knitting to find out. You may end up with a giant shawl as well. And loads of socks.

Sam Wallis

Am looking forward to you sending me a giant shawl, cos I'll need it to hide under after making such an idiot of myself in English. I wish I knew why he got into fights at his last school.

Gemma Smith

Do you think LOYL's a criminal? You could visit him in prison. You wouldn't have to compete with any other girls, and you could make sure your hair was at its best for every visit. He'd have to love you then, despite your Occasional Wind Problem.

Sam Wallis
Don't think he's a criminal. Got to go now.
Have the urge to dress Scuzzball as a baseball player.

Gemma Smith
Enjoy yourself. I'll get on with knitting your hat and scarf set. Am assuming you have an abnormally large head, to be on the safe side.

I chuckled to myself for at least half an hour after her last comment, then checked in the mirror. Just in case. I really don't want to have to add "Giant head" to my Negatives list. Things are bad enough.

On Saturday morning I did what I've been doing every Saturday morning for years with Gemma, and now am getting used to doing on my own. I went to the local stables, which are just a short cycle ride out of town.

POSITIVES
- I get to be around horses, which is good because horses are fab.

* I meet other people who love horses.

NEGATIVES
* I get covered in horse muck and get all smelly and disgusting.
* Cleaning out stables is knackering.

It's odd going to the stables without Gems. But at least everything else I love is the same.

The stable owner, Sheila, is no-nonsense and often quite grumpy, but she's really a softy underneath. I'm convinced that she likes horses more than she likes people. She strides about in her husband Stan's spare trousers and an old jumper.

Sheila was already leading the horses out when I got there. She lifted her hand in greeting. A group of excited little girls were waiting in the paddock, their parents helping them on with their riding hats.

My job's to muck out any stables Sheila hasn't finished, while she does the riding lessons for the paying clients. I also put out the feed and clean whatever equipment she's left out.

I was about halfway through my mucking out when I stopped for a rest. I was leaning against the stable door looking down at the paddock when I recognized a woman with long brown hair in a ponytail.

It was David Matthieson's mother! She was with a little

girl who was very cute and had wavy blonde hair. The girl looked so excited I guessed this must be her first-ever riding lesson.

This was incredible. Fate was bringing me and David Matthieson together somehow. First he was in two of my classes and now here were his mother and sister at the stables! Maybe I hadn't blown it completely after all. Maybe, if I could get his sister to like me, there was a chance he would think I was great too and overlook the recent embarrassing episodes.

I rushed the rest of my work, flinging straw around like a lunatic and working up a sweat in my efforts to finish before the riding lessons were over.

Finally I was done, and I hurried over to the paddock. David Matthieson's sister had just got off her horse and her mother was helping her take her riding hat off.

"Did you enjoy that?" I said brightly, giving her my best smile.

She fixed me with a hard stare. "Why do you have straw in your hair? And *why* is your face so wet and red and shiny?"

"I'm sorry," said David Matthieson's mum, embarrassed. "Jessica, why don't you tell the nice girl about how much you enjoyed your first riding lesson?"

"No," Jessica said, crossing her arms, "I don't talk to people who SMELL!"

Her mum looked totally mortified. And then I made it all worse. I just couldn't help myself.

"That suits me fine," I said, "because I don't talk to *brats*!"

"Well, really!" I heard David Matthieson's mum say, as I stomped off grumpily.

I bumped into Sheila.

"Are you OK?" she asked.

"No," I said, "I just called your newest pupil a brat, because she told me I smelled."

"Seems fair enough to me," said Sheila.

"Well, I'm sorry," I said.

"Go for a ride," advised Sheila, "it'll clear your head."

Sheila is a very wise woman.

Riding Pepper did help. I always find it easier to think when I'm out with her. We're lucky where we live; there's so much green space around our town. Loads of bridleways and beautiful views.

I wished I hadn't spoken back so quickly to David Matthieson's sister. I mean, what's the use of trying to score points with a seven-year-old? What was I trying to prove? I wish life was simpler, like it is for Pepper. She doesn't care what people say; she's content to get out and stretch her legs in the sunshine. In my next life I'd like to come back as a horse in Sheila's stables.

After I groomed Pepper I had a cup of tea with Sheila in her huge and messy kitchen. Cats and Labradors wandered around. She rummaged in a cupboard and dug out a packet of biscuits.

"Sorry I lost my temper with that little girl," I said. "They'll probably not come back now."

"Oh, they're coming back," said Sheila. "Her mum's signed her up for ten lessons!"

After our cup of tea, it was time for Sheila and me to have our session with Lucy.

Lucy, who's seventeen, has a type of cerebral palsy, which means she's got muscle spasms she can't control. She's been doing really well since she started with us last year, and she gets better every week. Some people have thought that Lucy's my older sister, because she has similar blonde hair to mine, though her eyes are blue instead of hazel.

It was a beautiful, sunny spring morning. Lucy rode well round the paddock, managing some of the turns and guiding the horse she was on by herself.

"You're so much more confident than you were a year ago," I encouraged her as I helped her dismount.

Lucy grimaced. She sometimes grimaces slightly before she talks, because it can be a real effort for her to get every word out.

"Thanks. Today's been good. But – I'll never be able to ride like you can," she said, "because of my stupid arms and legs."

"I think you're doing brilliantly," I said. "Look at you! Who'd have thought you'd be doing this? When you first came here you were too frightened even to get on a horse! Remember?"

"I suppose so," acknowledged Lucy, looking pleased. When Lucy smiles, she looks a million times prettier than when she's frowning.

Afterwards we had our usual chat and cup of tea in Sheila's kitchen. Lucy's doing her A-levels and was telling us all about her revision schedule, which seems to involve hours and hours of studying.

"It sounds horrendous," I said.

"It's not so bad," said Lucy. "It's – all about breaking things down into manageable chunks, that's what they say. Anyway, I need to get good grades."

Lucy is hoping to get into university to study law. She's a real brainiac.

"It's not the same – without Gemma," she said, sadly, as she was leaving.

"I know," I agreed. It isn't.

I decided to go to the bakery on my way home, to get some cakes to cheer Mum up. She seemed so tired from work and was still disappointed about her anniversary, even if she was trying not to show it. I was parking my bike when I saw Cat walking towards me, together with her band, Mr Bleaney.

Out of school uniform she looked even more stunning. She was wearing a purple cut-off T-shirt with a design of a pair of bright red lips on it, with a denim miniskirt and purple tights. She had on loads of black leather bracelets and was wearing a long scarf round her neck, which was black with silver through it. Eyeliner emphasized her brown eyes. She looked amazing. The rest of the band was dressed similarly to her, but mostly in black.

Then I realized what I must look like. I was wearing my

old, supposedly ironic pink sweatshirt with a picture of a horse's head on the front, and I was covered from head to toe in muck. I was in my worst old jodhpurs and boots. I put my hand up to my hair and felt the straw that David's sister Jessica had mentioned. I knew that I must look worse than terrible.

I turned and leaned over the bike, pretending to be checking the brakes. I know nothing about the brakes of a bike, but I needed an excuse to be facing away from the band. I didn't want to meet them looking the way I did.

"Hello, Sam!" said Cat as they approached. She seemed pleased to see me.

"Hello," I said, still with my back to them, and with my head down. I gave a little wave and then ducked into the bakery before she could stop and make introductions. When I was sure they'd gone past, I stuck my head out and looked after them. They were all laughing together and one of the boys put his arm round Cat. Out of nowhere I felt a little pang of envy.

Part of me suddenly thought: *Everybody thinks that Cat looks great. Loads of boys always pay her attention. Maybe if I looked totally, amazingly fantastic like that, David Matthieson would want to go out with me.*

In the bakery I bought four custard tarts, Mum's favourites. Then I cycled home, thinking all the way about how I could possibly manage to look half as good as Cat.

I also thought quite a lot about David Matthieson. I

can't help myself. It's like I can't get him out of my head.

I've never felt this way about anybody. I keep thinking about stupid things, like how his eyes crinkle at the corners when he smiles, and the way his arms look when his sleeves are rolled up. I have this feeling all the time that I want to be near him. Then, when I *am* near him, I feel completely tongue-tied.

It's a miracle I didn't drive my bike into a tree on the way home, I was so busy daydreaming about David Matthieson.

"Sam! You *know* I'm on a diet!" said Mum, who was ironing while watching TV. But she ate a custard tart anyway. She's got no will power. Ryan ate two without even asking. No wonder he has spots.

I went up to my room and looked in the mirror. It was worse than I thought. I saw the sweatshirt, the jodhpurs, the straw-filled hair and the sweaty face. Then I compared that image to what Cat looked like. It was not a comparison that did me any favours.

That was the moment I decided once and for all that I had to change my image, and fast.

Gemma Smith

I have BIG NEWS!!! I have found out Shona and Elaine's secret about where they meet boys. In six weeks there's a huge Highland Games on our island!! Apparently cos it's got lots of space, people come and camp and stay the whole weekend. There's a beach party on the Saturday night with live music. And there are THOUSANDS of boys! They come for the tug of war and tossing the caber and stuff like that, so they all have giant muscles. Hee heeee!

I AM SO EXCITED!!!!! It's going to be the best weekend EVER. But six weeks, it seems forever. How can I wait that long?

Sam Wallis

I'm SO PLEASED for you! At last you have something to look forward to apart from knitting. I thought that you really might throw yourself into the sea. I just feel sorry for all those big strong boys; they don't know what's waiting for them. LOL. When you see them, you might be so excited you'll start barking like a dog. This could, I warn you, put some of them off.

Things not progressing well here. Just getting worse. Met LOML's mum and sister. His sister told me that I smelled, and I called her a brat. Now I don't think his mum likes me either – can't think why (!!!).

By the way, Lucy says it's not the same without you. I need you to be honest. That pink sweatshirt with the horse's head on it I wear for mucking out. It's not the best look, is it?

Gemma Smith

You called his sister a brat? What else are you going to do to put him off? You might as well just walk up to him while gnawing on a giant hunk of meat. Just to make sure.

Tell Lucy I miss her too.

What's wrong with the horse's head sweatshirt???? It's like *The Godfather* meets Barbie. That's why we like it, remember? You're *supposed* to wear it ironically.

Sam Wallis

Not sure if I can be ironic on my own.

MY STATUS

Sam Wallis

Loves being out with Pepper in the sunshine.

Gemma Smith and **Darcie Clelland**

like this.

Gemma Smith I miss the stables and Sheila and Stan, and Lucy.

Sam Wallis We ALL miss you, Gems.

Chapter Five

I was enjoying a lovely long lie-in on Sunday when I was rudely interrupted by the sound of arguing downstairs. Mum was trying to get Ryan to do some housework, saying, "If you live here, you have to contribute. You can't just use this house like it's a hotel." Ryan was responding with his usual "I didn't ask to be born, just leave me alone" routine.

I really don't think there is anyone in the whole universe who's quite as lazy as Ryan. He's a lazy, custard-tart stealing, fish-neglecting toad. Fact.

When I got downstairs, Mum was doing the vacuuming she'd wanted Ryan to do while Dad sat in his armchair reading the paper.

As I've said, our house is falling apart. Cupboard doors are hanging off, carpets are coming loose. Wallpaper is peeling off. My room still has furniture more suitable for a five-year-old – a tiny built-in white Formica wardrobe and dressing table still covered in Teletubbies stickers. But Dad's oblivious.

I sat down opposite him.

"Doesn't it bother you, letting Mum do all the housework?" I said.

He put down his paper and looked over at Mum, who was grimly vacuuming under the sofa cushions.

"She needs the exercise," Dad decided. "Besides, I have to rest now. I'm doing my stall at the farmers' market this afternoon. Actually, I could do with some help. Will you give me a hand, Smiler?"

Dad calls me Smiler when he's being extra nice to me, or if he wants something. It's been his nickname for me since I was a baby.

"*No way*, it's about time Ryan did something for a change," I complained.

"I'll pay you a tenner," Dad said.

I thought about Cat's cool T-shirt and leather bracelets and scarf.

"You're on."

So that afternoon I helped Dad set up his stall at the farmers' market. He had a huge green-and-white-striped gazebo and a special portable fridge unit, and an enormous trestle table. He also had a giant banner that said "WALLIS & SON ORGANIC BUTCHERS" and underneath "MEATY AND DELICIOUS!"

We got them all out of his van and set up.

Then Dad produced two bright green baseball caps. He'd obviously designed them himself and had them made. They had "MEATY AND DELICIOUS!" written in huge red letters on them, together with a really lame cartoon of a sausage with arms and legs and a smiley face. The sausage seemed to be dancing.

I couldn't believe Dad had had these hideous baseball caps specially made. He'd really outdone himself this time.

"You're not expecting me to wear *that*, are you?" I said.

"Yes," said Dad. "We're pushing our new line, aren't we? I need you to wear the cap and hand out the sausages, together with our price list. I'll be cooking them on the barbecue."

"No way!" I protested.

"Do you want the money or not?" said Dad.

Half an hour later, I was wearing the ridiculous dancing-sausage cap, holding out a tray of chipolata sausages with cocktail sticks poking out of them. I didn't need to offer them; people were queuing up to grab them once they smelled them cooking.

"One sausage per person," I found myself having to say. Dad was beaming from ear to ear.

"Now this is what we call a PR exercise!" he shouted over to me, delighted.

I was just pointing out to a particularly tiny and very greedy old lady that she'd already had two sausages when I saw something I really did not want to see. I saw David Matthieson with his mum and his bratty little sister at the other side of the market, and they were heading our way!

His mum was lingering at a stall that was selling nuts and seeds. Probably planning their nut roast for later. And here I was, standing with a platter of pieces of pig, wearing a cap saying "MEATY AND DELICIOUS" on it. Could it possibly get any worse?

"Dad!" I hissed.

He couldn't hear me over the sizzling sausages, and David and his family were approaching at quite a pace. I didn't know vegetarians could move so fast. In sheer desperation I took off the cap, stuck it on the old lady, and handed her the platter of sausages.

"Help me out for a minute and you can eat as many as you want. Knock yourself out!"

The old lady looked puzzled, but she took the tray and immediately helped herself to another couple of chipolatas. She was absolutely tiny, so I couldn't understand where she was putting them all.

I began to walk briskly away from the stall. I reckoned that if I turned left and then left again, I'd end up beside a fruit and vegetable stall. My plan was that I would pretend to be browsing and casually say hello to David.

In my rush, I knocked into the corner of an old, rickety trestle table. The table was groaning with home-made cakes, puddings and pies lovingly made by the local home-craft and baking society, who are slightly on the old and rickety side themselves.

The disaster unfolded in slow motion. First the table leg gave way when I nudged it. Then the whole table tilted.

Desperately, I grabbed the falling edge of the table, trying to hold it up. As I struggled not to drop it, Victoria sponges and chocolate double layer cakes shot towards me.

A lemon meringue pie hit me smack bang in the chest and slid down my front, followed by a large, jam-filled chocolate cake. Meringue, cream, runny sticky lemon filling and huge lumps of chocolate and jam cascaded down me.

A couple of the ladies on the stall ran round to help, and between us we got the table level again. Somebody brought a couple of crates to prop it up. Luckily, only the pie and a couple of cakes were spoiled, and the rest we managed to save.

The old ladies thanked me for my help, dabbing at me with their handkerchiefs, little knowing I was the one who'd caused the disaster in the first place. I graciously accepted their thanks, then walked on with as much dignity as I could summon in the circumstances, trying to look as if I always have huge amounts of lemon meringue pie and chocolate cake stuck to my front.

Which was when, of course, I bumped straight into David Matthieson, his mum and his sister.

POSITIVES

● NONE.

NEGATIVES

● TOO MANY to list.

Gemma Smith

OMG! OMG! OMG! That is about the WORST thing I've ever heard in my life. Your whole front a mass of lemon meringue pie and chocolate cake?

Sam Wallis

LOML's bratty sister said, "Look! It's that smelly girl from the stables, Mummy." And LOML's mum said, "Come along, Jessica, it's none of our business!" And he just looked puzzled and sort of repelled.

Gemma Smith

Wot did you do then? How did you get away from them?

Sam Wallis

I just smiled, as if I walk around covered in cake all the time. Then I legged it back to Dad's stall.

Gemma Smith

Wot did your dad say?????

Sam Wallis

He was furious because the old lady had eaten all the sausages instead of handing them out. He'd only just noticed that she wasn't me!

Gemma Smith

He couldn't tell the difference between you and a tiny old lady?

Sam Wallis

No!!!!!!!! She insisted on keeping the cap, which is OK as it will be free advertising to the pensioner age group. But Dad wouldn't give me my ten pounds because he said I'd deserted my post and let him down and cos I messed up his van by dripping chocolate icing all over my seat on the way home.

Gemma Smith

Disaster.

I spent the rest of Sunday in my bedroom shouting "Why me?" very loudly, and chatting online to Gemma about how much I now hated lemon meringue pie.

I woke on Monday morning with a feeling of dread, knowing I was going to have to face David Matthieson in history.

On the plus side, my hair behaved itself.

I hoped David hadn't told anyone about the incident at the market. It was unlikely he had – after all, he didn't seem to talk to anyone much. He just kept himself to himself.

I walked into the classroom and there he was. He looked up and grinned. His eyes did that crinkly thing. Inside, I melted.

Trying to act normally, I sat down and pretended to be very interested in my textbook. I opened it to a page showing someone being stretched on a rack. They didn't look too thrilled about it.

"Lost the cake, then?" he said, leaning over so that he was quite close to me. I could smell his shower gel. He didn't just look fantastic. He *smelled* fantastic too.

"Yeah," I muttered, still staring at the person being stretched on the rack, my face turning its usual predictable red colour. It occurred to me that David Matthieson must think my face is permanently like that. I bowed my head, trying to pretend that I was extremely interested in medieval torture.

"Pity," he said. "I liked the whole 'edible dress' thing. Very Lady Gaga."

I raised my eyes and looked at him and WHAM. It was there again, that feeling of nobody else existing in the world. Time standing still. A big whooshing feeling. A hundred gerbils tap-dancing in my stomach. That sort of thing. After what was probably only a few seconds (but of course it felt like an eternity), I could see David's lips were moving.

"Sorry, what?" I asked.

"I said, you're friends with Cat, right?" he repeated, looking at me intently.

I felt myself plummet back to Earth and land in my seat with a bump. Why was he asking me about Cat? Oh no. . . Of course, it was obvious. This is what always happens on TV when someone has a much more beautiful friend. I should have known.

Luckily, at that point, Scary Donovan began the lesson and I quickly looked back down at my book. The lesson went by in a blur. I was hugely relieved Scary Donovan did not ask me one of his quick-fire questions, because I don't think I could have given him a sensible answer. Not that I can in normal circumstances, if I'm honest. As soon as the bell rang I fled the classroom, banging into people on my way, which probably made me look as if I was desperate for the loo.

Why, when I like him so much, am I so keen to run away from him? I wish I could talk to him like a normal person, but then I don't want to have a conversation where he tells me how much he likes Cat. And I'm sure he does . . . everyone else seems to, after all.

At lunchtime Taylor didn't join us, so it was just me and Cat.

"What sort of girls did David Matthieson like, at Bredborough Secondary?" I asked.

"I don't know," said Cat, frowning in thought. "There was one girl who he was sort of linked to, but it was more her idea than his. She was pretty quiet, nothing out of the ordinary."

"Did he ever ask you out?" I had to know.

Cat looked surprised, and then laughed. "No way! That would have been so wrong! We're friends."

I was pleased to see that the idea genuinely seemed to amuse her. Which meant it had never crossed her mind. That didn't mean it hadn't crossed his, of course.

"I was thinking of changing my image," I said, casually. "I want to look more . . . mature."

Cat looked at me appraisingly. "Do you mean you want to be less casual and have more of a style?" she asked.

I was relieved that she seemed to understand what I was getting at.

"Yes," I said, "I just want to be taken more seriously."

"Then we should go shopping," suggested Cat.

"That would be brilliant." I couldn't help grinning. Someone to go shopping with. This was great. Just like I used to go with Gems.

Then I thought of something.

"I'm going late-night shopping with Mum in London later this week," I said. "Would you like to come? You could bring your mum too if you want. "

"I'd LOVE it!" said Cat.

At that moment we were interrupted by Tania Hamilton, who decided to stop by our table with Angela Murray in tow.

"Hello, losers," she said.

"Nice to see you too," I replied.

"I hear you're the new singer for Mr Bleaney," Tania said to Cat, looking her up and down with her usual sneering expression.

"Yeah," said Cat.

"What were they thinking?" said Tania. "I mean, they were great as they were; what do they need a girl singer for?"

They walked on, leaving Cat looking upset.

"Take no notice of her," I told Cat, "she's like that with

everyone. She's just jealous of you."

"OK," said Cat, but she still looked shaken. I was surprised. I hadn't expected Cat to be affected by Tania. In my mind Cat was so self-assured, I thought she'd take someone like Tania in her stride.

"Would you like to go into town after school? We could go to a cafe?" I asked her. I didn't like the idea of her walking home on her own, feeling down.

"I'd love to," said Cat, "but I can't today. I've got to meet up with the band. Maybe tomorrow?"

"OK," I said, "and really, just ignore Tania. That's what I do."

On the way home from school I was so inspired by the idea of going shopping with Cat, I blew most of my weekly allowance on three glossy fashion magazines. I decided that if I was going to get my look right, research was essential. Of course Mum was as interested in the magazines as I was, so we ended up reading them together at the kitchen table.

"I think I need a new look," said Mum.

It was strange, I thought. There I was wanting a new look to get David Matthieson's attention, and Mum was thinking the same thing . . . probably in the hope of getting Dad's attention. I wondered if either of us would have any luck.

Later on, I found a message from Gems.

Gemma Smith

Hope it wasn't too bad seeing LOYL today at school.
I haven't laughed so much since I left. You're the only
person I've ever met who could get yourself into a
situation like that. Miss you loads.

Maybe you need to give up on David Matthieson for a
while, at least till he forgets about the cake incident
and your Occasional Wind Problem. Concentrate on
improving your ironic sweatshirt wearing skills
instead.

Gems xxx

Here I was making plans to change my image to try to get
his attention, and Gemma seemed to think there was no
hope, so I should keep wearing my old sweatshirt. I hoped
she was wrong. I couldn't forget how he smiled at me and
compared me to Lady Gaga. That had to be encouraging,
surely. But then again, he'd mentioned Cat.

When I went to bed, I took the fashion magazines with
me and stayed up far too late poring over the pictures of
the models, who looked effortlessly stunning in clothes I
could never imagine myself in. It was as if they lived in a
different world to me. None of them looked as if they
would be comfortable mucking out a stable. The words in
the magazines were so persuasive. "Let your clothes speak
for you", one article read. "Be incredible!" another
headline suggested. And then there was my absolute
favourite: "Embrace your inner diva".

I got to thinking as I lay there in bed. What do my clothes say, if they are speaking for me? Probably "Hopeless scruff-bag".

I miss Gems loads. But I don't want to follow her advice and wear my horse's head sweatshirt ironically on my own. If I can't be ironic with Gemma, I don't want to be ironic at all.

I've decided that I've got to move on. It's time for a brand-new Sam. Somebody with a bit of style about her. Someone with chutzpah, which is a word I've only recently learned, but I like it. I want to embrace my inner diva and be the sort of person David Matthieson would be proud to go out with, not a loser in jeans and a sweatshirt, with cake down her front.

MY STATUS
Sam Wallis
Had a fun weekend.
Penny Griffiths likes this.
Gemma Smith Heard you enjoyed loads of cake.
Tania Hamilton So the most fun thing you did all weekend was eat some cake. Saddo!

Chapter Six

Having a beautiful friend is, as I had suspected, not easy.

POSITIVES

* Boys swarm around, attracted by your friend's great beauty.
* I will never, ever become big-headed enough to wear the giant hat Gems is knitting me.

NEGATIVES

* Often the boys swarming around are boys like Taylor Griffen.
* I might as well be invisible.
* Boys are starting to ask me loads of questions about Cat, which is annoying.

"Where's Cat?" said Taylor, as soon as he sat down beside me in the lunch hall on Tuesday.

"Nice to see you too," I said. That is one of the perils of having a stunningly gorgeous friend, I was fast realizing. You are just a source of information for their many admirers. In the last week, it's not just David Matthieson who's been talking to me about Cat. Several boys who'd never bothered speaking to me before have struck up conversations and casually asked questions about her.

I was actually as disappointed as Taylor that Cat was not there. I wanted to ask her if she'd like to come round to my house to look at the magazines with me. I was hoping for some advice prior to our shopping trip. Also, I wanted to show her Scuzzball in his cowboy outfit, complete with miniature spurs. He looks magnificent.

Taylor went on – not in Ye Olde English, I'm glad to say – about how he'd been down to London with his mum at the weekend to audition for some TV commercial.

"They're looking for the new face of Puffy-Wheats," Taylor said excitedly. "If I get it, I'll be famous!"

Not long after, Cat arrived. I could tell she was approaching before she got to us just by seeing the reactions of some of the boys on nearby tables. One boy missed his mouth with his can of Coke and poured it down his front.

Taylor made a big thing of his Puffy-Wheats audition with Cat. You'd have thought he was up for the lead in the equivalent of *Harry Potter*. Cat was very enthusiastic and admiring, and Taylor actually began to puff up with pride. If he swelled up more, I thought, he wouldn't need a costume. He'd actually become a Puffy-Wheat.

As we left the lunch hall, Cat turned to me.

"I was wondering if you'd like to come to mine after school today. You could meet the band?"

I couldn't believe it: she was actually asking me to meet Mr Bleaney! Officially!

"Wow! I'd love to!" I stammered. This was great. But what on earth was I going to wear?

After school I rushed home and pulled out everything from my tiny, child-size chest of drawers and wardrobe. Of course, there was nothing suitable for wearing while hanging out with a band. I had nothing black, and nothing purple.

I owned about five pairs of jeans, all of them tatty and blue. Then there are my supposedly ironic T-shirts and sweatshirts, including: the horse's head sweatshirt; another sweatshirt with a photograph of three cute kittens on it; one with "Funky" written on it in silver glitter; a T-shirt with the *Little Miss Sunshine* cartoon and another T-shirt with a giant bright-yellow happy face emoticon.

Laying out my clothes on the bed, I could see the theme. Bright colours, cheesy images or slogans, lots of the colour pink. It had never seemed to matter before: they were just T-shirts and sweatshirts that made me happy, things that I could throw on. Now they looked like an enormous pile of rainbow-coloured embarrassment.

I selected the darkest blue jeans, and one of the few plain T-shirts I had, which had no design on it. Unfortunately, the T-shirt was bright pink (of course), but there was nothing I could do. Even if I'd had some money, which I didn't, there was no time to go to the shops.

I spent ages on my hair, hoping that if it looked good enough it would take attention away from my stupid clothes. But even though I managed to get it looking OK, it was just so . . . blonde. My hair, together with the pink T-shirt, just screamed "Barbie".

There was not one single thing, looking in the mirror, that I could find that I liked about what I was wearing. But – despite this horrific awakening – there was no way I was turning down Cat's invitation.

Cat's gran's – or rather, Cat and her mum's house was the other side of town, so I took my bike. When I saw the house, I remembered visiting it as a child. I remembered the red front door and the tubs of tumbling flowers on the doorstep.

Cat answered the door wearing black leggings with a long purple T-shirt over the top. Her hair was pulled up in a black scarf that had silver thread running through it, and she was wearing large hoop earrings.

"Glad you could make it," she said. "Everyone's out the back; I was just getting supplies." She held up a big bottle of Coke.

I followed her through the hall. The house still had her gran's old-fashioned furniture in it, but was also crammed with her mum's artwork, pictures of weird landscapes with red mountains and yellow moons and silhouettes of odd creatures that seemed half human, half animal.

The art was not the sort of thing my mum and dad would choose to have on their wall – it was too abstract and way out there – but I liked it because it was different to anything I'd ever seen. The house almost looked like a junk shop, it was so full of bits of art, ornaments and clutter. Cat saw me looking around.

"My gran liked to *collect* things," she said, raising an eyebrow and giving a rueful sort of smile.

"Is your mum at home?" I asked.

"Yes, she's in," said Cat. "She's in the attic, painting. She loses track of time. Sometimes she forgets to eat. So I get most of the house to myself."

"Wow! All that freedom must be amazing," I said.

Cat shrugged. "I suppose so," she said, not sounding enthusiastic about it.

We went through a messy kitchen, across a small patch of garden and into the large garden shed, where the band was practising.

They were working out an arrangement to back up a guitar solo, which was being played by a very skinny boy in even skinnier jeans. His legs were so thin, they looked like black shoelaces. His dyed black hair had a fringe so long and thick it totally covered his eyes, which made it even more incredible how good he was on the guitar, as I suspected he could hardly see it.

I stood, my mouth open, as he made his guitar sing effortlessly. He looked somehow vampire-like with his very pale skin. I noticed that instead of using a guitar pick, he'd just grown the fingernails on his right hand. They were varnished black, which I thought looked great. I wished I could grow my fingernails that long, but could imagine Sheila's reaction if I did. Long fingernails and horse manure just don't go together.

The drummer was wearing a striped red-and-blue T-shirt and faded black jeans, and his hair was even more spectacular than the lead guitarist's. It was bright ginger, all spiked up like a hedgehog. He looked over at me and gave a grin. The grin, together with his friendly twinkling eyes, made me warm to him immediately. He looked less of an emo than the others: he looked like he'd wandered in off the street and happened to be excellent at the drums, so he'd stayed.

Finally there was the bass guitarist, who was enormously tall – well over six feet – with long black hair with purple streaks in it and a permanent scowl. While the drummer and the lead guitarist were both cute, the bass guitarist looked terrifying. He seemed to be a couple of years older than the others – at least eighteen. He had a tattoo of a scorpion on his neck, and another of a lizard on his arm.

"The drummer's JJ," whispered Cat, as she poured Coke

into five mugs. "Watch out for him. He has a different girlfriend every week and knows how to turn on the charm. The one playing the solo, he's Dan. Isn't he *immense*? The guy on bass is Niv. He's not as scary as he looks, and I know it's hard to believe . . . but he's actually really shy."

I sat down on a packing crate and watched as they continued to rehearse. When they'd finished the song, they wandered over and had their drinks.

"This is my friend Sam," said Cat. Dan nodded, giving me a sort of half smile. The giant bass player Niv grunted, not meeting my eye. I felt incredibly self-conscious, and I knew that my face was fast turning as pink as my T-shirt.

"Pleased to meet you, Sam," said JJ, fixing me with his full attention, so that I felt I was the only person in the world. I wondered if this was what Cat meant about him turning on the charm.

They went back to rehearsing, and this time Cat sang. It was obvious they'd taken her on not just because she looked amazing but because she had a fantastic voice. They sang a song called "Looking for You", which was about looking for your soulmate and never finding them.

When I talked to Cat over a cup of tea after they'd gone, I found out that Dan was the main songwriter of the group.

"Although the others sometimes come up with the

words, or even entire songs," Cat said.

"I liked 'Looking for You' best," I said. "It was *so sad*, about searching and searching and never finding the right person. . ."

"It's just a song," Cat said. "Remember, it's not *true*! You're such a hopeless romantic!"

"You can talk!" I said. "You were always having pretend weddings where you got married to your cuddly elephant! Ha!"

At which point we both dissolved into laughter.

"Fair point," said Cat.

"Listen," I said, "I wanted to ask you, now that Taylor's not here . . . do you honestly think I might have a chance with David Matthieson? I don't even know if he likes me. Is this all a stupid idea?"

"Don't give up," said Cat. "If you like him, be friendly back. It might turn into something more, and it might not. Just relax about it. Be yourself."

I knew she was right. At least she thought I might have a chance. Maybe I wasn't being completely delusional.

"Do you promise there isn't something weird about him, or some other reason I shouldn't be interested?" I asked.

Cat laughed. "I promise," she said, "he's absolutely not a weirdo!"

At that moment, Cat's mum appeared downstairs. I couldn't believe how much she'd changed. When I was little, she was this petite, pretty woman. I remembered her having long, wavy fair hair and rosy cheeks.

Now she had lost some weight, which made her look even smaller. Her hair was now in a pixie cut which really suited her and made her pale blue eyes look enormous.

She'd always been attractive, but now I could see that Cat's mum was, like Cat, actually beautiful.

"Sam!" she said, giving me a hug. "You're all grown up! It's so good to see you again!"

I asked her about her painting.

"It's going well," she said. "I've got a few commissions, which is good. Thanks for asking."

Then she asked how Mum and Dad were, and I said that Mum was still working as a nurse, and Dad was still a butcher. We told her about the shopping trip and she said she'd love to come along.

Cat and her mum seemed to get along, but there was a slight feeling of tension in the way they spoke to each other. There wasn't the relaxed feeling between them that there is between me and my mum.

"Did you have a good time? It wasn't too boring for you?" Cat asked as I left.

"It was incredible," I said. "You're all going to be famous one day!"

Cat laughed. "Yes, us and about a million other bands playing in garden sheds!"

MY STATUS
Sam Wallis likes **Mr Bleaney**
Hanna Kermack Who's Mr Bleaney?
Tania Hamilton Only a band, you are SO out of touch.
Sam Wallis I heard them play, they are immense.
Gemma Smith I saw a sheep being sick yesterday.

Chapter Seven

Sam Wallis
What's up?

Gemma Smith
Saw another sheep being sick. Knitting. Counting down till the Highland Games. Actually, we had a fun night at Elaine's house. Most of the islanders went round and we all had a sing-song. Don't laugh!!!! Seriously, I enjoyed myself! People played musical instruments and some even recited poetry.

Sam Wallis
That sounds like my worst nightmare. Are you sure you are well? Have they brainwashed you?

Gemma Smith
Ha ha. Honestly, it was good.

Sam Wallis

Are you ordering lots of boy-magnetic clothes online yet? Or are you relying on your knitting skills????

Gemma Smith

Might go shopping on mainland soon.

Sam Wallis

Am going late-night shopping tonight in London with Mum and Cat and Cat's mum. My ironic sweatshirt wearing days are over.

Gemma Smith

No way. Why change a winning formula? And it's meant to be ME you go shopping with, not Cat!!! I am seething with jealousy. . .

Sam Wallis

You aren't here! Anyway you are busy knitting and singing (ha ha) with YOUR new BFs, so fair's fair. Have decided to become tres sophisticated and fashionable for the following reasons:

1) So that the next time I hang out with a band I won't embarrass myself by looking like I'm one of the Tweenies.
2) I am the only girl in Year 8 who seems to still wear the proper regulation uniform.
3) I want LOML to see me in a new light, not as a

potential friend but as a potential girlfriend. This is more likely to happen if I look less like a colour blind eight-year-old.

Come to think of it, it was YOU who got me to buy that horse's head sweatshirt in the first place!!!! You are obviously an evil, possibly Satanic influence.

Gemma Smith
Thank you. Wot do u mean "next time I hang out with a band"??? Talking about Mr Bleaney? Did you actually meet them??!?

Sam Wallis
Yes!!!!!! They were rehearsing at Cat's house.

Gemma Smith
It's all "Cat this" and "Cat that" with you. Humph. How's your mum, by the way?

Sam Wallis
Not good. Still all stressed compared to her usual happy self. She's just had a radical new haircut and colour (from mousey shoulder length to a blonde bob) and Dad didn't notice! It really suits her but I swear he didn't notice a thing!!! Which, Mum pointed out, means he must have stopped actually looking at her years ago. With that and giving her a bag of meat for her anniversary present,

Dad's not doing too well . . . in fact, they've had a couple of arguments recently, which isn't like them at all. I think that's why Mum's decided to go out and blow some money on herself tonight, to try to make him take notice of her.

Gemma Smith
Give her my love. Have a good time becoming sophisticated. Good luck on that one! LOL. By the way, you're not ordinary.

Sam Wallis
Miss you!

After my chat with Gemma, I went into London with Mum and Cat's mum and Cat.

We met at the train station, and Mum and Cat's mum had a big enormous hug, then proceeded to talk at full speed the whole way into London. It was good to see Mum so happy, reminiscing with Cat's mum about when me and Cat were little. Of course they had to tell all the most embarrassing stories, such as the summer when me and Cat ran around the garden naked.

I couldn't get over how much Mum's new haircut suited her. Getting rid of her greyish mousiness took years off her and she looked fantastic.

Of course, as soon as we got to Oxford Street, me and Cat and Mum and Cat's mum went in opposite directions.

I had a little bit of money with me, which I'd found in various money pots and jars around my bedroom. It was all stuffed into my bag, which I held close to me. I did not want to have my precious loot nicked.

Now this is the shocking part . . . Mum quietly slipped me five, yes FIVE, ten-pound notes before she disappeared, which totally surprised me. She's a strong believer in earning your own money, so this unexpected handout was totally out of character. I wondered what had come over her.

It was different, shopping with Cat instead of Gems. Usually me and Gems would be falling about laughing as we held inappropriate outfits against each other. But with Cat, it was a serious business. Every decision was a crucial one, and there was less time for joking around. Not that it wasn't fun shopping with her, I don't mean that. It's just that we were on a mission.

We decided to find me some good accessories and some darker clothing than my usual bright stuff. The first thing I bought was a black leather pleated bracelet, because loads of people in London seemed to be wearing them. Looking around, I felt like such a country bumpkin. I was sure that my clothes showed everyone who looked at me that I was from a town rather than a city. Cat, in contrast, fitted in perfectly. She looked incredibly stylish in a little black jacket with a dark red T-shirt underneath, the perfect jeans and fab jewellery.

In fact, I kept seeing girls of about my age walking past

who, like Cat, looked like they were from the pages of magazines. I began to get style envy, which I've never felt very strongly before.

With Cat acting as advisor, I got three pairs of thick black tights, a short black skirt and a pair of skinny black jeans. We felt that was a safe basis for my new look.

Next I got a pair of dark green shorts, to wear over tights. To go with them, I found a grey long-sleeved top with a silver design on it that was a complete bargain. We agreed that now I would at last look vaguely as if I was aware of fashion at parties, instead of clueless.

Then we hit the jackpot. We found a shop that sold all black and purple clothes, and it was really cheap! So I got two black T-shirts and a purple one. I also got a long black scarf that had purple glittery thread running through it, and a purple scarf with silver thread running through it. Cat got a few things too, including a little black dress which wasn't expensive, but which looked expensive on her.

In the last half hour before the shops closed I bought some black nail varnish, purple eyeshadow and black eyeliner. By the time I'd finished I was carrying three carrier bags and felt as if I'd had the biggest spending spree of my life. And everything was either grey, green, black or purple.

"You've got some great new stuff," said Cat approvingly. "David's *got* to be impressed!"

But my shopping spree was *nothing* compared to Mum's.

When we got to the underground, where we'd arranged to meet, Mum and Cat's mum were standing there. Cat's mum had one carrier bag, but Mum had about seven giant bags arranged in a circle all around her and a look of absolute glee on her face. No wonder she'd slipped me money – it was out of guilt, because she knew she was going to spoil herself massively. And I'm sure Cat's mum encouraged her every step of the way. That's what's so dangerous about shopping with a friend.

"Mum! You've gone *mad*!" I said on the train, as she pulled out item after item to show us. Actually, with Cat's mum's help, she'd chosen some good stuff, stuff that I could see would make her look good and flatter her figure.

"*And* I'm getting contact lenses!" she announced. "I'm sick of my glasses. It's time for a whole new me!"

"Quite right!" said Cat's mum. "Spoil yourself for a change. You deserve it!"

I wondered if Cat's mum was a good influence. When we finally got home, I thought Dad would keel over when he saw all her purchases. In fact, I'm sure he would have if he hadn't been sitting down.

"Bloody hell, Julie, what's all this for?" he said.

"It's my twentieth wedding anniversary present to me," said Mum. "And don't worry, it cost far less than it would have cost you to take me to Paris or Venice. So I'm not finished spending yet!"

And with that, she swept past him and up to their room,

probably to try on all her new clothes and strut around – much like I did in my bedroom.

I looked so different! I could not believe it, but suddenly I looked at least three years older without all my babyish pinks and blues. In my black T-shirt and black skinny jeans, I practised looking nonchalant in the mirror. In my new short skirt, purple scarf and black tights, I realized I might actually suit something else apart from blue jeans. I decided my look before had been "immature tomboy". Now it was going to be "stylish, feminine, sophisticated and edgy". David Matthieson would have to take notice now. *And* I could hang out with Cat without feeling embarrassed about what I was wearing.

I was uncertain about my make-up. I decided to experiment before I launched myself on the world. Somehow the black eyeliner looked too heavy. I wondered if it was because I was putting it on wrong. I wandered through to the bathroom to find some cotton wool to take it off when I met Ryan coming out of his room, no doubt to do one of his smash-and-grab raids on the fridge. He was in the middle of a guitar-playing frenzy; I could tell by the fact that his hair was standing on end and the wild look in his eye.

"Urrgh," he grunted. "You look weird." Which was the longest sentence he's said to me in months.

"Thanks," I said. To be told you look weird by a toad with sticking-up hair is pretty rich, really.

Gemma Smith
How did the clothes shopping go?

Sam Wallis
Fantastic. Whole new wardrobe. Whole new me!

Gemma Smith
Send me some pics immediately!

Sam Wallis
Will do.

I went into school the next morning wearing a normal school shirt but with my new short black skirt and thick black tights. I had on a tiny amount of eyeliner, not too much. I thought I'd better not risk overdoing it. I've been wearing mascara for ages (due to my blonde eyelashes), but the eyeliner is a new step and I wasn't sure if it suited me.

Taylor gave a loud, exaggerated wolf whistle when he saw me in the corridor, and I noticed a couple of other boys giving me a second glance who would normally not notice me. By lunchtime I was feeling pretty good about myself.

"Hey! Looking *good*!" said Cat, looking pleased that her advice had paid off.

"Have I put it together OK?" I asked her. "What about the eyeliner?"

"It's great," Cat reassured me.

So when I went into the Friday afternoon English class, I was sure David Matthieson would be impressed. The problem was, he didn't seem to notice that there was anything different about me. He just said "Hi, Sam" when I walked past his desk.

I was disappointed. But then when I looked behind me, he grinned at me. Whoosh! It was still there. On my side, anyway.

Towards the end of class, Tania Hamilton loudly made a few panda jokes about my eyeliner, and when I checked in the mirror after class I saw she was right. I'd rubbed my eyes and created a slight panda effect! No wonder David Matthieson hadn't looked blown away by my new look. He was probably wondering why I had two black eyes.

My bubble of self-confidence popped, and I felt quite flat and grumpy for the rest of the day.

I didn't have the heart to message Gemma when I got home, but instead I dressed Scuzzball in his clown costume, which always cheers me up. I do so love his angry little face. In the evening, I decided I needed to change my Facebook photo, so got poor Mum to take about fifty pictures of me in my new clothes in various poses.

"I don't think you suit so much black," Mum said, unhelpfully, "and do you need to wear that eyeliner? Doesn't it make your eyes look smaller?"

"Mum, you've *no idea*," I replied, "honestly!"

❋

On Saturday morning I went down to the stables, but didn't wear any of my new gear. I didn't want to ruin it. So it was back to the horse's head sweatshirt. When I walked in, I was surprised to see Sheila's husband Stan taking the riding lessons. Sheila was in the kitchen with her leg in a plaster cast. It turned out she'd fallen off her tractor and got a nasty fracture.

"I'm going to need you to do much more than usual," said Sheila, holding court with her leg up on a cushion. She was holding an enormous mug of tea. "I might need you to come down and help during the week as well, until I'm out of plaster."

I promised I'd do my best, but my heart sank. Without Gemma the workload was heavier anyway, and now with Sheila out of action it would be harder still. But I couldn't let her down.

After a marathon mucking-out session and a quick ride on Pepper, I was running behind and was late for my session with Lucy. She was waiting in her wheelchair by the paddock, playing Scrabble on her phone.

"You look tired," she said.

"I had to do double today because of Sheila's ankle. Stan had to do the lessons."

Lucy laughed, because she knows what Stan's like. He's a very quiet man, so he hardly says anything, and there's all these puzzled kids wondering what they're supposed to be doing.

"He was rubbish!" I went on. "Sheila ended up hobbling

out and leaning on the fence, shouting instructions. Poor Stan, he hasn't a clue."

The session with Lucy went well, and my tiredness dropped away as I saw how much she was enjoying herself. I found myself telling her all about David Matthieson, and Cat, and my recent shopping spree.

As I was helping Lucy off her horse, she looked closely at me.

"Have you been wearing eyeliner?" she asked.

"Yes," I said, "most of it's come off now."

She stared at me. "Not – sure if it suits you," she said.

Honestly, I thought. Why did everybody think they had a right to comment on my image? First Mum, now Lucy.

"Well, I thought I'd try out a new look," I said, defensively.

Lucy grimaced. "You don't need to look like Cat, whoever she is. You're pretty enough as you are."

"Six-year-olds can be pretty," I argued, "but I don't want to look like a six-year-old!"

Lucy shook her head, laughing. "You don't!" she said. "You look at least ten!"

When I got home, I had a grumpy message from Gemma.

Gemma Smith
Well, obviously you're far too busy prancing around in glittery scarves to tell me how your new look went down at school or send me the pics your promised? I

have to see your new profile pic along with everyone else!!! Not good. Are you now an emo? Are you going to burn all your ironic sweatshirts? I am presuming you are more interested in putting on eyeliner than messaging your BF...

Sam Wallis
Sorry.

Gemma Smith
Humph.

Sam Wallis
Grovel. Grovel.

Gemma Smith
Humph.

Sam Wallis
No excuse, except post-shopping exhaustion, and distraction due to going into school in new clothes. Yes, I did get some black clothes to try to balance all the colourful stuff I've got, and no, I'm NOT turning into an emo, I promise.

Gemma Smith
How did your new look go down at school?

Sam Wallis

Excellent. Wore black skirt to school with black tights. Felt weird, but good. Got some whistles due to my not-too-bad legs. Tania Hamilton called me a panda due to my eyeliner, even though it was just a tiny bit smudged and she wears loads of it herself so she can't talk.

Gemma Smith

Don't listen to Tania. You do have good legs. And your new photo is v. foxy. I might have to change mine to picture of myself in giant tartan shawl (of course).

Sam Wallis

So what's happening?

Gemma Smith

Do I really have to tell you about another sheep being sick? Either there is a sheep illness round here or they're all bulimic. Just assume that nothing ever happens here, unless I say otherwise. . .

Sam Wallis

At least you have the Games coming up.

Gemma Smith

Shona and Elaine are getting very excited. I think I am getting v. desperate. Actually, I do have news. Went with Mum and Dad to mainland today. All I could do was stare at boys, cos I'd not seen any my age for so long.

Sam Wallis

Wot did you get?

Gemma Smith

Some new jeans, and a dress, and two tops (one of which is not at all ironic and is black, in your honour). And some boots, and new underwear.

Sam Wallis

That's great. Nice of your mum.

Gemma Smith

She just feels guilty because they're shutting me up on this island like a nun. I nearly wept when we got back on the boat!! Here I am back on the island, and it's a Saturday night, and there is nowhere to go. I am so bored. A sheep being sick is starting to be the highlight of my day.

Sam Wallis

Sorry I was out of touch. Rubbish of me.

Gemma Smith

You're totally forgiven, but you've got to tell me EVERYTHING that's going on. I'm relying on you to bring some excitement to my life. OK??????

Sam Wallis

If it's any comfort, it's Saturday night here, and I'm not going anywhere. I have no life and have probably put LOML off me even more by smudging my new eyeliner and looking like a demented panda. Which I can add to the list of ways I've been putting him off me, like walking up to him covered in cake, and playing Juliet to Taylor's Romeo. At least he doesn't know my dad's a butcher . . . well, I don't think he knows. OMG he probably does know. Would be just my luck.

Gemma Smith

It's lucky your dad's van is just plain white and doesn't have dancing sausages on it.

Sam Wallis

Sheila's broken her ankle in a fall off a tractor, so she can't do loads of her work. I ended up staying twice as long as usual, and it was knackering.

Mum's acting oddly. She's gone out tonight without saying where she's going, and she's all dressed up in her new clothes and wearing her new contact lenses. Maybe she's having an affair!! Dad's not at all bothered, but is watching TV, drinking beer and eating peanuts. This is what happens when you are middle-aged. I don't ever want to get old and end up like them.

> **Gemma Smith**
>
> Sheila breaking her ankle, your mum having an affair. That's more like it. Keep telling me what's going on! I love it!

MY STATUS
Sam Wallis
Bought loads of new clothes in London.
Penny Griffiths, **Gemma Smith** and 3 others like this.
Hanna Kermack Like your new skirt.
Taylor Griffen Good to see you've actually got legs.
Penny Griffiths Our scruffy tomboy Sam is turning into a young lady!
Tania Hamilton Sam Wallis is a lay-deeeeeeeeeeee!
Sam Wallis Very funny.
Tania Hamilton Lay-deeeeeeeeeeeeeeeeeeeeeeee eeeeeeeeeeeeeeee!

Honestly, I can't believe Auntie Penny! It's like she sits and works out the most, the MOST inappropriate and embarrassing comment she can make.

Chapter Eight

On Sunday morning at breakfast Mum was looking fantastic. With her fab new hair and without her glasses (which weren't very flattering), I'd say she's taken ten years off. Not that Dad seemed to notice.

She revealed she'd been visiting Cat's mum the night before.

"I thought I'd catch up with Eileen," she said to Dad, casually. "She came shopping with us last week. I'd have mentioned it to you, but you were too busy having a heart attack about what I bought."

"Eileen *Malloy*?" Dad put down his knife and fork, which meant that he was surprised.

"Yes," said Mum. "She's back in Greenfields. She's painting full time. I've asked her and Catrina to come round on Saturday night."

"Good," said Dad, slightly doubtfully, "that's great."

Gemma Smith

All that seems to be happening here is my dad looking at seals and talking about seals, while Mum writes about milk churns and talks about milk churns. I wish my mum would go out all dressed up and mysterious like yours, but if she did it would only be to talk to the sheep.

Shona and Elaine have both for some reason dyed their hair burgundy and are suggesting that I do the same. What do you think? I think we'd look stupid at the Highland Games if we ALL have burgundy hair. Also, Mum would kill me. She'd rather I was wearing one of those bonnets you see in old paintings, and a big white linen apron. The other day she suggested that I learn to make goat's cheese with her. You see, we have three goats, and she's all into the idea of using the milk (which is disgusting) to make cheese (which would be even more disgusting, I imagine).

I told her that I thought we were living in the twenty-first century. Now she's not speaking to me. My parents are not normal. Help.

Sam Wallis

Ring ChildLine immediately. Btw, do you like my new Facebook pics, seriously?

Gemma Smith

Of course I do, you look lush. Is Cat on Facebook? I don't see her on your friends list.

Sam Wallis

I looked her up but she's not there. She must be the only person I've ever met who's not on it.

Gemma Smith

What are you planning in your campaign to get LOYL? Have you looked for him in the library yet?

It's been raining here <u>too much</u>. There's no point in even trying to straighten my hair, it ends up curly the minute I step out of the door. Mum's still going on about goat's cheese. Kill me, please.

On a positive note, Shona's got a karaoke thing and we had the best time the other night, me, her and Elaine. You should have heard my Katy Perry impression.

Sam Wallis

I can just imagine you making cheese. Well, I can imagine the expression of boredom or horror (not sure which) on your face anyway.

No, I have NOT stalked LOML to the library. Wasn't it you who suggested I leave things for a while?! He smiled at me in history again this morning. But he's probably just being friendly out of pity. I couldn't concentrate on the lesson. I am <u>so</u> going to fail history this year.

On Monday I was glad Tania wasn't in my history class, so she couldn't make any more remarks about my image. Towards the end of the lesson, David Matthieson leaned over and whispered: "I hope you don't pay any attention to Tania. I quite like pandas. They're sort of cute. *And* they're an endangered species."

He was smiling, with that twinkle in his eyes. I found myself gulping like a fish drowning on the shore, unable to come up with anything sensible in response. So I just grinned back at him, hopelessly, thinking how lovely he was.

At lunch, I found myself sighing repeatedly. Taylor and Cat were chatting, but I wasn't listening. I was thinking about David Matthieson and wondering if I should take his saying he liked pandas as encouragement.

"Sam! Aren't you listening?" Cat was saying.

"Sorry, I'm in a dream world," I said, truthfully.

"It looks like I'm coming round yours on Saturday night," Cat said.

"I know," I replied.

Cat smiled. "Hey! It'll be just like old times."

I smiled back. It would be. Except I doubted we'd be sitting up in my room having tea parties this time.

In English the next day, Taylor made some remark about me having long legs, which made me feel incredibly self-conscious. Especially when I noticed David Matthieson looking over. Suddenly I wished I was back in my safe trousers, the old Sam.

"Sam is a bit of a beanpole," said Tania loudly and dismissively, "so she would have long legs. Like a giraffe."

Great, first I was a panda and now I was a giraffe. I caught David Matthieson's eye and he gave me one of his fabulous smiles, but it was as if his eyes were saying "Don't listen to her". Which was comforting. Cat was right, he was decent. I just hoped he wouldn't now tell me he liked giraffes.

I didn't follow him to the library or anything so stalkerish. I just continued the week living up to the promise of keeping Gemma updated on the boring details of my life. It was good to get her messages; they made me laugh, and miss her.

On Friday at lunchtime I was chatting to Taylor and Cat and told them about Tania's remark in English, saying I looked like a giraffe.

Cat laughed. "Yes, David told me. It's hilarious. First she calls you a panda and then a giraffe. She really hasn't a clue!"

"You spoke to David?" I said, wondering when. He seemed to be avoiding everybody outside classes, and Cat wasn't in any of them with him.

"He popped in last night while the band were there," said Cat, casually. "He usually does cos he knows JJ."

I was surprised. Then I wondered why I was surprised. After all, Cat had made no secret of the fact they were friends.

"Next time he comes by, do you want me to sound him out properly about you?" suggested Cat. "I think he might like you. He did mention you a few times."

"No!" I almost shouted. I was horrified at the idea of David Matthieson knowing about my crush. And I wasn't as sure as Cat that he liked me, not if he was popping by to see her. "I don't want him to know I like him. Please, you mustn't tell him."

"OK, OK," laughed Cat.

As I walked home that day, I didn't know what to think. David Matthieson and Cat were getting together outside school on a regular basis. It was becoming more obvious he liked her. How could she not see it?

Gemma Smith
Mum has got all the goat's-cheese-making equipment set up in the garden shed. She is so excited.
Three and a half weeks until the Highland Games. It feels more like three and a half years. Will it never happen?

Sam Wallis
Glad my mum doesn't do stuff like that to me. I think your parents would like to live in the eighteenth century.
Found out something interesting about LOML. Cat told me. Apparently there are a couple of Mr Bleaney songs with lyrics by him!!!! He knows the drummer,

JJ! It was LOML who got Cat the audition to be their singer.

The more she tells me, the more I think it's so odd they don't hang out together at school, since they sort of know each other from before and they've got music and Mr Bleaney in common. Cat says she's as puzzled as me that he's spending all his spare time hiding in the library. She seems to think she can get him to join us for lunch.

Eeek!!!!!!!!!!!!!!!! I'll probably get something stuck between my teeth. Like a huge slice of ham. Just as he walks in.

He went round to her house the other day. Apparently he goes round all the time. Not sure what to think. Just because Cat doesn't think of him as anything but a friend doesn't mean he's not in love with her. It's highly likely given that most of the boys in our year are pining for her.

Gemma Smith

I wish I could tell you that you're wrong, but I don't know him and you'd have to see them together to try to work it out.

Mum and me finished making a big batch of goat's cheese today. It was amazing! I really enjoyed it! We took it to our nearest neighbours, who are called the McFarlanes, and they thought it was good. So we might be supplying the island shop and post office, as nobody else is making goat's cheese.

When I read Gemma's message on Saturday morning, I laughed so much at the idea of her making goats cheese and enjoying it, I nearly fell off the bed. It made it bearable, going back to the stables for yet another week of double duty.

Sam Wallis

Knackered. Been at stables and done twice as much, like last week. Saw LOML's bratty sister and she stuck her tongue out at me. She is so cheeky! I stuck mine out back and did a cross-eyed face to show her she doesn't intimidate me. Mum is fussing about tidying the house for Cat and her mum coming round tonight, and I'm the only one who's helping her. Dad and Ryan are so lazy it's disgusting.
Got to go, Mum's shouting for me to put crisps in bowls. Have put Scuzzball in his disco diva outfit. He's not happy about it, but he looks fab. Will put picture up tomorrow.

Poor Mum got herself in a real flap about Cat and her mum coming round. She made a risotto, then set the table all fancy with proper place mats and the best cutlery. Dad was annoyed about the risotto, since it departed from the meat and two veg tradition of our household, but Mum told him to get over himself and take out the rubbish, and he was surprisingly obedient for once.

Ryan announced he was going to eat in his room and play guitar with Matthew, and Mum said he certainly was not and that Matthew would have to go home and Ryan was going to eat with us. Ryan repeated that Matthew was staying. Mum got very annoyed and shouted until Matthew left and Ryan stormed back to his room and slammed the door. It was the usual family bliss in the Wallis household.

Dad disappeared and appeared again in his favourite Hawaiian shirt, which screams "I'm a fun guy!". He wears it at every opportunity.

The doorbell rang, and there was Cat and her mum. Cat was in a very short denim skirt with a baggy black top. She was wearing purple eyeshadow to match her nail varnish and about fifty thin silver bangles. Totally striking. Her mum was looking radiant too.

Mum called Ryan to come downstairs, and he appeared, wearing his *I'm not going to enjoy this* face. Which suddenly changed as soon as he saw Cat. Into a love-sick puppy dog face. I should have guessed that would happen.

We went through to the lounge and sat down on the sofas, feeling slightly awkward.

"Would you like a crisp? They're sea salt and balsamic vinegar. I think you'll like them." Ryan materialized, creepily, beside Cat, brandishing a bowl of crisps. Mum and I stared at each other in disbelief.

"What would you like to drink, Eileen?" Dad stood like

an overenthusiastic Hawaiian wine waiter, clasping his hands.

"Just an orange juice, thanks, Rob," said Cat's mum.

Dad chose the fanciest glass he could find and added orange juice, ice, a cocktail umbrella, a slice of orange *and* a twirly straw. Then he presented it ceremoniously to Cat's mum and sat down. Nobody else had a drink, but Dad didn't seem to notice.

This is typical of my dad. He likes to be a fantastic host, and he runs around after guests like they are VIPs, flattering them and fetching things for them, while ignoring Mum completely. He's just such a people person, he can't help himself. But it always annoys her.

Then Dad had to do his flattery bit, and of all the things to notice, he had to notice Cat's mum's hair.

"I like your new haircut," he said. "It suits you."

"I wouldn't mind a glass of wine, please, Robert," Mum interrupted icily, "and I think the girls would like something to drink too. Maybe a Coke?"

I knew Dad was in trouble because she called him Robert rather than Rob. He knew it too. He actually looked scared.

Ryan leapt up. "Would you like a Coke?" he asked Cat, as if he was asking her to marry him.

"Yes," she said, with a shy smile, "and I'm sure Sam would too."

"Coming right up," he cried, enthusiastically rushing off to the kitchen. He returned with two Cokes, shoving mine at me and presenting Cat with hers as if he were Sir Walter Raleigh presenting Queen Elizabeth I with a potato, or some tobacco, or whatever it was.

Dad brought a glass of wine for Mum, who was now, I could tell by her false smile, silently seething with rage.

Luckily Mum recovered herself enough to chat politely to Cat's mum. They talked about their new haircuts, telling each other that they looked younger – in fact, even younger than when they first met. Mums can be totally delusional, especially when they are with other mums. They all tell each other how gorgeous they are. It's collective blindness.

"How's Joe?" interrupted Dad, as tactless as ever.

There was an awkward pause.

"He's fine," said Cat's mum. "In fact, I'm relieved to say he's now got himself a girlfriend. They're *much* better suited than we ever were. She's called Carol, isn't she, Cat?"

"Yeah," said Cat, noncommittal.

Mum and Dad smiled, relieved Cat's mum was not going to do the whole "he's a complete monster and he's ruined my life" bit.

"Shall we go through and eat?" suggested Mum in that slightly posh voice she only ever uses when we're entertaining guests. We all trooped through, including Ryan.

"I thought you were eating in your room," I said. This was only me telling the truth.

Ryan threw me a murderous look as he placed himself

opposite Cat. I felt sorry for her, having to eat her risotto while looking at his spotty face. But she didn't seem to mind; in fact, she was smiling shyly at him.

Suddenly I remembered how, when we were little, she used to like Ryan. It was not like a proper crush, just that sort of constant gazing and copying and trying to impress that younger children do when they look up to older children. I'm sure she even told me she was going to marry him when she grew up. In some of her pretend marriage ceremonies with her cuddly elephant, I am certain that the elephant was playing the part of Ryan.

I looked over at them again and thought, *No, this cannot be happening.* Cat was looking at Ryan as if he were good-looking and interesting. It was insane. I mean, couldn't she see that he was a hideous, boil-covered toad? What do you do if your friend has a crush on your brother?

POSITIVES

* YOUR FRIENd WANTS TO COME OVER TO YOUR house all the time, which saves you the trouble of having to go over to hers.

NEGATIVES

* YOUR bROTHER bECOMES EVEN MORE UNbEARAbLE because he NOW thinks he is a god.

- your friend is more interested in talking about your brother than talking to you.
- It could lead to them getting married and that would just be too weird.

Dad sat opposite Cat's mum and was being all jolly and jokey.

I went through to the kitchen to help Mum serve up the food. She looked annoyed.

"He's only doing his Perfect Host act as usual," I pointed out.

"I know," Mum said, in a tired voice. "It would just be nice if he did a Perfect Husband act."

Not even Scuzzball in his afro disco diva wig and medallion seemed to cheer her up.

Chapter Nine

> **Sam Wallis**
> It's late but had to tell you about tonight. OMG! Ryan was like a love-struck idiot about Cat. Cat seemed to like it too much. And Dad annoyed Mum by being so busy being entertaining and hospitable, he ignored her completely. Again.

> **Gemma Smith**
> Hideous!

On Sunday morning, I decided to go for a run. I like to run at least once a week, because I'm on the athletics team at school and I'm trying to improve my time for cross-country. I really pushed myself and did about three miles. I was feeling good about my achievement until, yards from home, I ran past David Matthieson and his mum and sister, who were getting into their car outside their house.

I couldn't believe they were out and about so early. My face was the colour of an overripe tomato and I was dripping with sweat. I was sweating in a way that only a middle-aged, overweight man would usually sweat. My hair was actually sticking to my head.

Worse still, I was wearing an old and nasty pair of grey baggy jogging bottoms and a bright yellow T-shirt with the slogan "Girl Power" on it.

David Matthieson raised his hand in greeting. I half-raised mine in return, aware of the giant sweat patches under my arms.

"Look, it's the smelly girl," said Jessica, waving.

Sam Wallis
LOML saw me running!

Gemma Smith
Oh no! I suppose you were sweating. At least he now knows how sporty you are. He might like that. What else is going on?

Sam Wallis
Not much else. There's a music festival called Plastic Moon the weekend after next – the same weekend as your Highland Games. Cat's going to it cos Mr Bleaney are playing, but there's NO WAY Mum would let me go so I'm not even bothering asking her. Besides, she's so stressy these days cos of her work. Lots of homework to do.

Same as usual, really. How's the goat's-cheese-making and knitting?

Gemma Smith
Going well. Cheese-making's quite good fun, once you get the hang of it. Don't worry, I'm not wearing an apron and bonnet. Not yet. Mum's giving me fifty per cent of the profits. With that and my scarves I'm going to be rich!!! I am going to be a BIG CHEESE!!!!!

Sam Wallis
HAHAHAHAHAHAHAHA HAHAHAHAHAHAHAHAHA HAHAHA! That is so funny.

Gemma Smith
I know. I am hilarious.

Sam Wallis
Goats are funny enough, but you making goat's cheese is funnier still.

Gemma Smith
You can talk . . . don't get me started on your quirks. . .

The week continued with only one exciting thing happening, which was actually pretty big by the standards of Grungefields. Taylor Griffen found out he was the new face of Puffy-Wheats!!!

"You watch," he told Cat and me at lunch, "everybody's going to want to have lunch with me once I'm famous. But don't worry, I'll stick with you. After all, you like me for who I am, not just my soon-to-be celebrity status."

We had to smile. Taylor had always gone from table to table at lunchtime, gossiping and joking and being the life and soul of the party, never sitting regularly with one group of people. But now he was our regular lunch buddy, and I actually didn't mind that it was probably because he was captivated with Cat. Lunch was fun with him around, telling us of his plans for international stardom. And at least he'd stopped talking in Ye Olde English all the time.

David Matthieson kept on eating his lunch in the library. Now he'd seen me running, I was pretty sure that all hope was lost. Mum was still really stressed out because of having to do long days at work. And Dad was being, well, Dad.

The only thing different was the way Ryan was behaving. I could hear him now in the bathroom, doing his new skincare regime, which involved about twenty lotions and creams and him being locked in there for hours on end. I tried to block out the scrubbing and sloshing noises and went downstairs.

No Mum. Which was odd, as she's normally home way before this. I wondered if she was round at Cat's mum's house, as she'd gone round there on Tuesday. But she'd rung me on my mobile to tell me where she was. I decided to ring her, but it went straight to answerphone.

Dad came home.

"No sign of your mum?" he asked.

Dad joked about Mum being up to no good and tried her mobile with no luck. Then as it got later, he stopped joking.

I had the idea to go round to Nosy Norah's to see if she knew anything. She wasn't in.

"Have you got Mrs Malloy's phone number?" Dad asked.

Cat's mum had no idea where Mum was.

Eventually Dad rang one of Mum's workmates, Val. When he came off the phone, he looked serious.

"Your mum didn't go into work today. In fact, Val said she wasn't expecting her to be in for a while. Something about her being on leave."

"Try her mobile again," suggested Ryan, who was reeking of antiseptic face wash. Dad rang the number. This time, Mum answered.

"Julie! Where are you!" said Dad. Then he just listened, and said "OK," and then "What the. . ." and then he hung up.

He sat down at the kitchen table looking surprised and annoyed.

"Your mum's gone on a Caribbean cruise!" he said. "With Norah from next door, of all people. Norah won it in some competition. I *can't believe* she's gone off for a *whole two weeks* without telling us . . . with *no warning*! Did she think we'd try to stop her?"

"What about our dinner?" said Ryan, which was typical. And which probably explained why Mum had gone off without telling us.

I was in shock. This was so completely unlike Mum. But I had to stand up for her with Dad and Ryan.

"I think it's *fantastic*," I said defiantly. "It's about time she had a break."

"Well, she's got a strange way of going about it," muttered Dad, still wearing a confused and slightly ill-done-to expression. "I'm going out."

He put his jacket on and slammed out of the house. Dad never gets angry, probably because he usually gets his way, so it was quite strange to see.

Ryan stood up.

"Mid-life crisis," he muttered. I wondered if he was referring to Mum or Dad. It probably applied to both of them.

He got some bread out of the breadbin and stuck it in the toaster.

"What are you doing?" I asked.

"Making myself something to eat," he said.

I went up to my room and sat down on the bed, still in shock. I tried to think about the Positives and Negatives of the situation.

POSITIVES

⊛ MUM at last getting the break she needs from her life of drudgery. Serves Dad and Ryan right.

⊛ MUM, being MUM, will feel so guilty about actually enjoying herself for a change, she'll spoil me rotten when she gets back.

⊛ MUM is not around to check up on me and tell me to do my homework.

NEGATIVES

⊛ Nobody to do the shopping, laundry, tidying up.

⊛ Everything's going to fall apart, possibly on a global scale.

⊛ She didn't take me with her.

⊛ She might like it so much, she'll never come back.

So the prize was genuine, after all. All expenses paid. And Norah chose Mum to share it with. But it was so odd that Mum didn't tell us in advance. Like Dad said, did she think we'd have stopped her?

The truth was, maybe we *would* have stopped her, without meaning to. Ryan and Dad would have been horrified at the idea of Mum going off, leaving them to find their own pants. And in all honesty, I probably would have been horrified at the idea of being left with Ryan and Dad.

Then I saw a note propped up on my dressing table. It was from Mum.

Dear Sam,

I am so, so sorry I went off without saying goodbye. I didn't know what your dad would say so it just seemed easier to go. I have been so stressed recently, I really need a break. I know you'll be fine because you are a sensible girl. If things get bad, just go and stay with Cat. Eileen won't mind.

One piece of advice. Your dad and Ryan are going to try to get you to do everything. Don't fall into that trap. It's time they learned to cope on their own, so don't so much as peel one potato for them and whatever you do, DON'T do their washing. I've left you some money in your sock drawer. Look after yourself; I'll be home soon.

Love you,

Mum xxxxxxx

I rushed to my sock drawer. There, nestled between my socks, was a roll of bills, tied with an elastic band. An actual wad of cash! I unrolled it and counted it. Mum had left me a *hundred pounds*! All at once! I'd never held so much cash. It was obviously for me to use for lunch money and in case Dad didn't buy healthy food, but all I could think about was the Plastic Moon Festival Cat had been going on about. And here I was with a hundred pounds, and no Mum to stop me going! This, I decided, was fate.

Chapter Ten

Sam Wallis

Mum has gone to the Caribbean with Nosy Norah from next door! She says it's because she is stressed. She just went without any warning! Dad is furious.

Gemma Smith

OMG!!!!! Are you OK?

Sam Wallis

I'm fine. Was too busy at the stables this morning to dwell on things. And then I had a good long chat to Lucy about it and she made me feel better because she pointed out that it's only two weeks and it's better if my mum sorts herself out and gets less stressy. Which is true.

House is already a disaster zone: mugs and biscuit wrappers strewn around, Ryan's pants on the landing at the top of the stairs, because actually lifting the lid of the laundry basket seems to be beyond him. The sink is full of greasy plates and a burnt frying pan from Dad's attempt at breakfast. Mum's only been gone for just over a day!!

Gemma Smith

That's terrible.

Sam Wallis

I hope it makes Dad and Ryan finally realize how much she did for them. I think they're expecting me to take over. As if.

Gemma Smith

Ugh. Poor you. Don't you DARE start cleaning up! That's what they're counting on. Be strong. Just put a clothes peg on your nose.

Sam Wallis

Enough about me, how are you?

Gemma Smith

Feeling disgustingly excited about the Highland Games. Wondering if I'm some sort of mad boy-chasing maniac. I never used to be like this, and now I'm just as bad as Shona and Elaine. The closer it gets to the big weekend, the faster they are knitting, with excitement. Their knitting needles are going to burst into flames if they don't watch out.

Gemma Smith

Am very jealous that you can go to your festival on your own, or with Cat or whoever instead of WITH YOUR PARENTS!!! Yes, the milk churn queen and the king of seals are planning to be there, of course, especially as they are now so friendly with all the neighbours. Luckily it is such a big event, I'll be able to shake them off and lose myself in the crowds.

On Monday I put on black nail varnish, even though it's against school regulations. There was no Mum to spot it, and it's not like Dad would notice something like that. Of course Scary Donovan picked up on it in history.

"I'm sure you know the rules on nail varnish?" he said as he passed my desk. "If I see that again, it's detention."

"Sorry, Mr Donovan," I said, in what I hoped was a sarcastic voice. I could feel David Matthieson's eyes on me but didn't want to blush, so I glared down at my book, trying to look defiant and annoyed.

When I was leaving the classroom, he caught me up.

"Are you OK?" he asked. "Only you don't seem . . . yourself."

"I'm fine," I said, then I blurted out: "My mum walked out on Friday."

"*What?*" David looked shocked. All of his attention was focused on me.

I have to admit, I liked it. This sudden interest. Which I hope in some way explains why I did what I did. Which was not to actually lie. . .

"They've been arguing for ages," I said in a sad voice. "Mum's been unhappy. I don't blame her for going. She just left; she didn't even say goodbye."

"Where is she now?" he asked.

"With a friend," I said, which was true. I just didn't mention that she was on a cruise in the Caribbean and was coming home in two weeks.

He was radiating concern.

"I've been through it. It's tough," David said. "If you need to talk, come and see me. I'm in the library most lunch hours."

Then he patted me on the shoulder. A friendly sort of a pat. But I didn't care.

"Thanks," I said, hardly able to believe my luck. First, the money and the possibility of the festival . . . now David Matthieson asking me to come and talk to him! Which could, if you were particularly delusional, be seen as practically a date. After the past few weeks of him not seeming at all interested, this was fantastic. It was all I could do to stop myself grinning like a Cheshire cat. I walked off, trying to look as traumatized and miserable as I could.

I carried on with the deception at lunchtime. I knew

Cat would already know or would soon find out that Mum had gone off on a cruise with our neighbour. But I made sure that she and Taylor had the impression that she might not return because she was so fed up. I was so convincing, I convinced myself.

"I had no idea things were so bad," said Cat, squeezing my arm.

"It was *awful*," I lied.

"So she actually threw a *rib-eye steak* at him!" gasped Taylor, after my ever-so-slightly reinvented version of their anniversary. He was loving the drama of the situation, of course.

"You *poor thing!*" said Cat, finally. "I can't understand how you've been able to put on such a brave face. You've seemed so genuinely ... happy. And to think that underneath you were practically dying inside!"

I tried to look as if I was dying inside. This was difficult. Firstly, I am not a good actress. In school plays I've usually been a tree, or one of a troupe of friendly forest creatures, or something equally in the background. Secondly, my face seems to arrange itself in a goofy smile most of the time. Which is why Dad calls me "Smiler". I decided I'd have to practise looking miserable in the mirror when I got home.

I am now officially living a lie!

POSITIVES
⦿ Attention from David Matthieson.

- Cat bought me a bar of chocolate. Feel slightly guilty about that. But not enough that I couldn't eat it. Oink. Oink.

NEGATIVES

- Just to be pretending such a thing means that I am very tragic, and should get a life.
- I'm bound to get found out sooner or later.

Things in the Wallis household got worse as the week progressed. Mugs of tea were growing a sheen of mould. Stuff in the fridge was stinking. The washing basket was overflowing with Dad and Ryan's clothes. (I was hand-washing my own in the bathroom sink and drying it on the radiator in my bedroom.) I bought some bread with some of the money from Mum and had barely made myself beans on toast when Ryan fell on the rest of the loaf like a hungry wolf.

In the evenings, Dad brought home fish and chips. This was good for the first couple of nights, but soon even Ryan was looking less than enthusiastic. Then Dad brought home some sausages and cooked them, but forgot all about vegetables. Ryan commented that he didn't realize we were going on the Atkins diet and Dad got all annoyed and went off in a huff.

Taylor wasn't around on Tuesday lunchtime, so Cat took the opportunity to talk to me about her parents' divorce.

"I know how you feel, Sam," she said, "so you can talk to me about it. Mum and Dad had all those huge fights before he eventually left. Please, please don't tell anyone this. The truth is, Mum was drinking too much. She had a real problem."

Cat looked really vulnerable all of a sudden. I thought how hard it must have been for her to tell me this. Instinctively I reached over and squeezed her hand.

"It must have been horrendous," I said. Now I could see what Cat meant when she said her mum was messed up. "Is she OK now?"

"Yes," said Cat. "But part of me is still angry with her, for being rubbish for so long. It was horrible; it was like I had to be her parent. I still blame her for the split up, although I know that's not fair. I mean, part of why she was drinking was that she wasn't happy, and some of that was Dad's fault. It's so complicated, parents' relationships."

"I know, isn't it?" I said. But I felt bad, because what had happened with her parents was real, whereas I'd exaggerated what was happening with mine beyond recognition. Cat had genuinely been through a very tough time. Whereas I was a complete fraud.

I wondered if I was doing all this lying because I felt that my life was so boring and uninteresting. Mum and Dad's petty squabbles and Dad's obsession with rib-eye was not the stuff of teenage trauma at all. It was laughable and pathetic. But once you start to tell lies, it's hard to stop. Cat and Taylor and David honestly believed my story. I couldn't go back on it now, could I?

On Wednesday I got up the courage to visit David Matthieson in the library. He was doing his maths homework while eating a peanut butter sandwich.

"Hi," I whispered. He looked up and gave me his fab smile. My knees felt wobbly. I told myself to get a grip. Luckily he motioned to me to sit next to him.

"How're you doing?" he said, looking at me in a searching way. I tried to look miserable.

"OK," I said, "I'm . . . coping."

"You've got to remember it's not your fault," he said, looking deep into my eyes. This made me think that he must have felt it was his fault when his parents split up. Which made me feel so sad for him, I didn't need to act any more.

"Really," he said, "there's nothing you could have done."

I honestly thought that I might burst into tears, I felt so guilty about the fact that I was completely exaggerating my situation just to get his attention when he'd obviously had a rubbish time. And then to think what Cat had been through . . . I didn't deserve an ounce of their sympathy.

"I've got to go," I said, getting to my feet. "Thanks."

Then I did what I seemed to do best where he was concerned. I ran away.

Cat was delighted when I said I could go to the Plastic Moon Festival.

"That's *fantastic*!" she enthused. "I can get you a

backstage pass – I've got a bunch because we're playing. You can travel down in the bus and camp with all of us. Mum's coming as a chaperone, but she's pretty relaxed."

"Fantastic!" I said. "It sounds perfect!"

Gemma Smith

One week and three days, which is ten days. TEN DAYS to go. Have found out that loads of people camp, and in the evening there is a barbecue on the beach and people stay up all night dancing and listening to music!!!
To keep myself busy, and because it's sort of fun, I am knitting and making cheese like a maniac.

Sam Wallis

I'm worried about you.

Gemma Smith

YOU can talk!!! From what you messaged me about what you've told David Matthieson, I'm surprised that you are not in flames due to your pants being on fire. . .

On Friday, I went back to the library. I was unable to keep myself away from David Matthieson, not when I knew he wanted to talk to me *and* be sympathetic and lovely.

"How're you managing?" he asked.

I sighed. "Dad's so *angry*!" I said.

This was actually true. Dad was absolutely livid. He kept going on about how Mum was using up two whole weeks of her annual leave, and how selfish she was. He stomped around, tripping over stuff he and Ryan had left lying about and then swearing and kicking things across the floor.

He kicked the vacuum cleaner (which I'd left out as a hint), his own football boots, Ryan's bag of unwashed and very smelly PE kit *and* a plate with leftover fish and chips on it. The plate broke, and shards of broken china plus a few remnants of fish and chips were now trodden into the lounge carpet, adding to the growing health and safety crisis around us.

"What about you," David asked, "are *you* angry?"

He was really good! Like a trained counsellor.

"Yes," I said, "I'm really, really angry. I'm so angry I could. . ."

I tried to think of something that you would want to do if you were very angry. The problem was, I wasn't at all angry.

". . .I could . . . throw my rucksack!" I said, lamely.

"Why don't you?" David Matthieson suggested. "It might make you feel better."

This was awkward; I wasn't used to doing that sort of thing. Still, I thought I'd better go along with it. I picked up my rucksack and hurled it as hard as I could. Narrowly missing the heads of three Year 7s (it was lucky they ducked), the rucksack sailed majestically across the library and landed on the desk of Mrs Sutcliffe, the librarian, with a loud thump, scattering papers and tipping over her cup of coffee.

"I didn't mean *right now*!" he whispered, trying not to laugh. "I meant when you got home!"

Mrs Sutcliffe pointed at the rucksack.

"Who threw this?" she shouted. This meant she was officially breaking library rules. Which I personally thought was *not* setting a good example. . .

At this point, I started to laugh uncontrollably. My shoulders shook. I had to cover my mouth with my hand. Tears came to my eyes.

David stood up.

"I threw it," he said.

"My office, immediately!" said Mrs Sutcliffe, turning on her heel. David smiled a sheepish smile at me, and followed her.

I managed to get out of the library, and staggered off down the corridor, still laughing.

"Where were you?" demanded Cat, when I arrived late in the lunch hall. I'd managed to stop laughing, and now I had a dopey smile on my face.

"In the library," I said dreamily.

"With David Matthieson?"

"Yes," I said, "and he did a noble deed for me."

Cat looked interested. "What noble deed?"

"He took the blame for me throwing my rucksack at the librarian."

Now Cat looked puzzled.

"Why were you. . .?" she began.

"Never mind that," I said. "The point is, he took the blame."

I sighed deeply, and I could feel that my cheeks were flushed.

"That's really promising!" said Cat, delighted. " We're definitely going to have to get him to start having lunch with us."

Sam Wallis

I've got big news. The best news! Today LOML got into trouble, because of <u>me</u>.

Gemma Smith

Tell all.

Sam Wallis

It's a long story but it was sort of his fault too, because he made me throw my rucksack – well, he didn't make me, but I misunderstood him and threw it and then he said he'd done it . . . so he got banned from the library for a week and detention.

Gemma Smith

Why was he making you throw your rucksack?

Sam Wallis

To get rid of my anger about Mum leaving. But he hadn't meant me to do it in the library.

Gemma Smith

Anger therapy???? You should be ashamed of yourself. Letting him think you're from a broken home while your mum's sunning herself in the Caribbean.

Sam Wallis

I have no shame. I don't care.

Gemma Smith

So he took the blame for you. That's promising.

Sam Wallis

There's more. I hung about at school till after detention so I could thank him and we got talking again and I told him I was going to the festival and GUESS WHAT? He's going too! Unfortunately with his mum and sister, but at least he's going! We talked about it all the way home. Yes, we <u>walked home together</u>!!!!!

I'm so happy, I don't care about the house being disgusting, or having to eat bacon and raw carrot for dinner.

Gemma Smith

Just be careful. Don't fall for him too much.

Gemma was right. I would have to be careful. But in the meantime I just couldn't help feeling really hopeful.

MY STATUS
Sam Wallis
Is going to the **Plastic Moon Festival**.
Penny Griffiths and **Gemma Smith** like this.
Tania Hamilton Big deal. Got my ticket weeks ago.
Hanna Kermack I'm SOOOOOOO jealous. My parents would NEVER let me go.
Penny Griffiths I remember going to Glastonbury in the 1980s. I had lovely purple dungarees.

Chapter Eleven

I overslept on Saturday morning, and when I woke up I thought that I must still be dreaming. I could hear the sound of vacuuming! I lay there puzzling for a while, deciding that it must be the TV. But when I went downstairs, there was Dad in Mum's pink flowery apron, vacuuming away while Ryan was washing up! For a moment I thought that it must be some sort of hallucination. I blinked a couple of times, but they were still doing housework.

"Good morning, Smiler!" said Dad, back to his old cheerful self. "We're having a clean up!"

"I can see that," I said. "How much are you paying him?" I nodded towards Ryan.

"Not a sausage," said Dad, in butcher-speak. "By the way, your friend Cat rang when you were still asleep. She's coming over."

So that explained the sudden industry. They couldn't bear the thought of the beautiful Cat knowing what hideous slobs they were.

"Ha!" I said, bitterly, heading for the toaster. I wondered what Cat was coming round for. She knew I went to help Sheila on a Saturday morning. We'd barely have time for a cup of tea before I had to go out. Still, I was pleased that she was coming round.

I was halfway through my second slice of toast when the doorbell rang. It was Cat, looking stunning as usual in a long black and grey stripy cardigan and skinny jeans.

"Would you like a cup of tea?" asked Ryan, smiling at her. To see Ryan smile was unnerving, as it looked unnatural and wrong.

"I'd love one," said Cat. "Sam, I thought I'd pop round to see if you'd like to come to the cinema later – I've got two-for-one tickets for *Rose of Destiny*. I thought we could go to the matinee showing."

Rose of Destiny is a new film about some girl called Rose who's dying and fulfilling all her final wishes. It's apparently a real weep-fest, not my sort of thing at all. I was relieved I had a genuine excuse to not go.

"Sorry," I said, "I'll probably still be at the stables. Sheila's got some extra work for me today."

"*I'll* go with you," said Ryan, in a slightly strangled voice. Despite him being my brother, and the fact that because of this I wish for horrible things to happen to him on a daily basis, I actually felt sorry for him at that moment. His scrubbed but still spotty face all hopeful. I steeled myself for Cat's polite "No, thank you".

"That'd be great!" Cat said, grinning from ear to ear. "But are you sure it's your sort of thing? It's about a girl who's dying."

"Is it?" said Ryan, also grinning. "Sounds good!"

Yes, he *actually said* that he thought that a film about a girl dying sounded good. That's the sort of stupid thing boys say when they fancy someone enough. Another example would be: "Yes, I'd *love* to visit your incontinent and bearded Great-aunt Irene with you."

So they were going to go to the cinema together. Cat and Ryan. This was just too strange for words. I felt like I'd slipped into some sort of alternate reality where things looked similar but were actually completely different.

POSITIVES

- If the movie is lame enough it will be such a horrible experience they'll never want to go out together again.
- Can't think of anything else remotely positive about it.

NEGATIVES

- The dark environment could encourage snogging, which is unthinkably horrific.
- It could actually be seen as being a date.
- Where does that leave ME?

At the stables, I told Sheila about Ryan and Cat going to the movies together. She can always be relied upon to come out with some sort of no-nonsense wisdom.

"He's my brother and she's my friend! It's *so wrong*!" I said.

"You can't fight hormones," said Sheila, offering me the packet of biscuits. "It's human nature. We're no different to baboons. The mating instinct, it's a very powerful thing."

Stan, who never speaks but agrees with whatever Sheila says, nodded wisely.

"Euuugh! Now I feel really *sick*!" I said, waving away the custard creams in disgust.

All the way through my work and then throughout helping Lucy in her lesson, I couldn't get Sheila's remark about baboons out of my head.

"You – seem distracted, Sam," remarked Lucy, who was practising turns and doing pretty well at it too.

"Sorry," I said, "it's just Cat has gone to the pictures with my brother. I don't know what she sees in him. He's a complete *toad*."

"I think he's quite good-looking," said Lucy. She's been round our house a couple of times and has met Ryan.

"Is everybody going *mad*?" I asked nobody in particular.

When I got home, I went to make myself a sandwich, pleased to come in to a reasonably tidy house. I opened the kitchen cupboard to get a plate, and out fell a load of junk! Ryan must have just scooped up everything that was on the kitchen table – which ranged from some dirty dishes to a pair of his stinking socks – and shoved them out of sight.

Then, as I sat down on the sofa in the lounge, I felt as if I was sitting higher up than normal. When I lifted the sofa cushion, I found more dirty socks, a discarded pizza carton, some computer games, two old newspapers and the greasy frying pan. So this had been Dad and Ryan's idea of tidying up. I should have guessed.

At that moment, the phone rang. When I answered I could just hear a crackly interference noise at first; then I heard Mum's voice.

"Sam! Are you all right? Is everything OK?" She sounded worried. She probably thought the house would have burned down by now.

"Great!" I lied. "We're all fine. How's the cruise?"

"It's *wonderful*! Most of our fellow passengers are American. We've met this lovely couple called Marty and Dee, and we sit at their table at dinner. Norah won the karaoke competition last night. She sang 'Sex Bomb' by Tom Jones."

"That's fantastic," I said, trying very hard not to think of Nosy Norah singing "Sex Bomb".

"How did your dad take it?" she asked, the worried note creeping into her voice again.

"He was grumpy at first, but he'll be OK," I reassured her. "He did some vacuuming this morning."

There was a silence at the other end of the line; Mum was apparently in a state of deep shock, which was understandable. When she recovered, she made me swear that I was OK, and I made her promise to enjoy herself, and then she was gone. Off with Nosy Norah to a salsa class.

Mum said that the instructor, who was a "very nice young man", was helping her to work on her hip movements. I decided not to pass on that nugget of information to Dad.

Her last words were, "See you next Saturday!"

Oops! And I'd be off at the festival. I was well and truly rumbled.

I decided I'd still go. After all, if Mum could go off to the Caribbean, I could do my own thing too. Couldn't I?

Gemma Smith

Less than a week, less than a week, less than a week!!!!!!!!!!!!!!

Guess what? It's LESS THAN A WEEK! This time next week you'll be at your festival and I'll be at the Highland Games with lots of fit Scottish boys. All we need to do now is pray we don't get big spot breakouts. Have been knitting scarves like mad. They don't look bad, if I do say so myself. Mum is so proud. She says that I'd have been very successful in the olden days, with my own "cottage industry". I suppose it is satisfying to know you could survive with your own skills. OMG. Listen to me!!!!

Sam Wallis

It's so exciting! Am also excited about the weekend. Just ran upstairs to check for spots, all clear for now. Might do a face pack. Guess what? Ryan and Cat are at the cinema TOGETHER.

Gemma Smith

Ouch! Brother-and-friend-cinema-shocker! You don't need to worry that I'd ever do that, he's so not my type. She may be stunning and a great singer and cool . . . but she likes your brother, so she is definitely deeply flawed!!!! Hahahahahahahahahahahahahahaha hahahahahahahahaha!

By the way, DON'T do face pack! It'll bring out your spots, not make them better. I mean, they'll get worse first.

Sam Wallis

Too late. Have face pack on right now. So will be a giant mass of spots at the festival.

I am glad Ryan's not your type because if YOU went out with him I'd have to kill you both. I must check his room to see if he's got any books titled *How to Hypnotize Girls into Thinking You Are Attractive When Really You Look Like a Toad*. I am in deep shock and may need counselling about this. What else is happening up there?

Gemma Smith

Since the cheese-making we seem to be being accepted into the community as useful people. We got invited to another singalong at Elaine's house. And I'm going to start helping out at the post office (if you can call it that). Got to go now, my scarves won't finish themselves. Love and xxxxxxxxxxxxxxxxxxxxxxs

I was disappointed when Gems went off to knit her scarves; I had been enjoying the chat.

I wondered if I'd be able to adapt to such a remote existence. Maybe, I thought, we get used to anything. Maybe anything seems normal after a while.

While I was waiting for Ryan and maybe Cat to come back, I decided to try to distract myself with some clothes organizing. Then I had a long chat to Sid the knitted monkey about life. Sid is an extremely good listener. Then I tried putting on purple nail varnish but with black stripes. It didn't work at all, so I took it all off and just did black nail varnish.

At this point, I heard Dad come in. He's often up at the shop on a Saturday afternoon to keep an eye on things. Still annoyed by his and Ryan's rubbish tidying up, I ran downstairs and pointed my Finger of Accusation at the frying pan and rubbish under the sofa cushion.

"That must have been your brother," said Dad, sitting on the other side of the sofa rather than dealing with the mess. "Be a love and put on the kettle, would you?" He opened the newspaper and settled himself back with a satisfied Dad-type grunt.

"No. If you can't clear up properly, I'm *not* making you tea!" I said.

Dad produced one of his all-too-familiar red stripy bags from seemingly nowhere. It was filled with sausages.

"Then you'll not be wanting your share of *these*, will you?" he replied, looking all smug.

I took a deep breath. "You think that walking in here with some sausages or a pork chop or two from your shop means that me and Mum have to run around after you like you're the Emperor of . . . of . . . like you're the *Emperor of Meat*! Well, we've had enough! No wonder Mum's run off. She's sick of being your slave! *She works too!* I have *school* all day! You're not the only one who gets tired and wants to sit down!"

I turned to stomp off to my room, but my path was blocked by Cat and Ryan standing in the doorway of the kitchen, grinning. They must have heard me call Dad the "Emperor of Meat". Which I have to admit is a pretty good new name for him.

MY STATUS
Sam Wallis
Thinks that hiding socks, pizza containers and frying pans under sofa cushions is NOT proper tidying up.
Gemma Smith, Hanna Kermack and **Darcie Clelland** like this.
Hanna Kermack LOL
Tania Hamilton Get over it. Have you got OCD or wot?

Chapter Twelve

After my tirade at Dad, Cat asked me back to hers, to have tea and sit in on an evening rehearsal with Mr Bleaney.

As we left, she flung a casual "See you" over her shoulder at Ryan. He looked slightly gutted and I almost felt sorry for him for a brief moment. It didn't last.

Cat's mum was wearing dungarees splattered with paint, and there was even paint in her hair. She let us go up to her attic to see her latest artwork, a huge canvas with three red mountains, the silhouette of what looked like a deer, and a blue crescent moon in a yellow sky, with a shaft of white moonlight shining down across the landscape.

"It's really great!" I said. "And it's *huge!*"

"It's for the lobby of an office building in London," Cat's mum explained. "I hope they'll like it as much as you do."

"They will!" I assured her.

After our quiche and salad, which was fantastic after all the rubbish Dad's been inflicting on us, we sat out in the garden waiting for the band to arrive, as it was a warm evening.

Now that I knew what had happened with Cat's mum's drink problem, it made me look at her differently. It's easy to assume that adults are all sorted and infallible. But Cat's mum obviously wasn't. She was mended now, but she'd been broken.

I could tell by the way she and Cat were with each other that they didn't have the usual mother-daughter relationship. There was too much history, and still some tensions. Now I understood why.

"How's your mum?" asked Cat's mum. "What's this I hear about her going on a cruise?"

I blushed crimson, because I was sure Cat would have passed on my exaggerations about Mum and Dad's fights.

"Oh, yeah, she's gone with our next-door neighbour," I said.

"I'm sorry if things have been difficult," Cat's mum remarked. So Cat had told her about rib-eye steaks flying across our kitchen. Oops. I began to realize that it's true what they say: your lies will usually come back to haunt you.

"Are you looking forward to the Plastic Moon Festival next weekend?" Cat's mum added. "I can't wait!"

"Yes, I'm looking forward to it," I said. "Thanks for letting me tag along."

Cat's mum smiled. "It's a pleasure. I'll give your dad a ring about arrangements."

Again, I blushed in dismay. I'd not even mentioned my plans to Dad. I'd been planning to tell him I was staying with Cat and not to mention the festival at all.

Why, I thought, did everything have to be so complicated?

When Cat's mum disappeared back upstairs to paint, I confessed that I'd not told Dad about the festival.

"I don't suppose I've got a remote hope of going now," I lamented. "I don't even want to go home, I'm so annoyed with him. The last thing I need is to have to ask him a favour."

"I've got an idea," said Cat.

Cat rang home for me, and to my surprise, she asked to speak to Ryan. While she was waiting for Dad to put him on the line, she winked at me!

"Hi, Ryan," she said. "Listen, I've got a favour to ask. Sam wants to come to the Plastic Moon Festival next weekend, but she's worried your dad will say no. Do you think you could persuade him?"

There was silence while Cat listened to Ryan.

"Well, that might be a good idea. So you think he'd say yes, then? OK. See you later."

She hung up and gave me a big thumbs-up sign. I stared at her in amazement.

"But . . . what. . .?" I stammered.

"Ryan thinks he can swing it," said Cat, "but the catch is, he's going to have to come too. He thinks it's the only way your dad will agree, if he's there to keep an eye on you."

145

I shook my head. "You know the real reason he suddenly wants to go, of course?" I said.

Cat gave a little pleased smile.

"I don't understand what on earth you could possibly see in him," I said. "No offence, but he's a disgusting, smelly, lazy, obnoxious, giant-footed, toad-faced, Frankenstein-monster-like, antisocial *moron*. Of course, that's just my opinion."

Cat smiled again. "You're his sister," she said. "You're bound to feel that way. Don't worry, it's nothing serious."

Suddenly I felt as if we weren't both thirteen. I felt as if Cat was sixteen and I was eleven. Maybe, I thought, I should grow up a little, to match my new more mature image.

At that moment the doorbell rang. It was JJ, Dan and Niv ready to rehearse. I was pleased that they didn't seem annoyed that I was there. I was also pleased that I wasn't wearing a pink T-shirt and jeans this time. I was in my black jeans and purple T-shirt, with my black scarf.

Niv was still silent, but Dan became more chatty as the evening went on and I saw a new side to him. While he looks like a dreamer, he is actually very sure of what he wants, which is to make music his career one way or another.

"If Mr Bleaney doesn't make it," he said, "I'll try to sell my songs. I might even study music production."

JJ is more doing it for fun – at least that's the impression I got. He's hoping the band will do well, but if things don't happen, he says he'd like to be a music journalist or do some sort of writing for a living. They all seem to have an idea of where they are going, which made me think about the fact that I don't really know what I want to do with my life yet. Maybe when I'm sixteen, like them, I'll have more of an idea.

"My brother, Ryan, plays guitar," I said, "but he and his friend haven't got a band together. They talk about it, but they don't actually do it."

"Some people only ever play in their rooms," said Dan, "but there's nothing wrong with that. It's great they play at all. Music's good for the soul."

I liked that idea, that music was good for the soul. It occurred to me that Cat and Ryan *and* David Matthieson were all into music. Maybe, I decided, I should learn an instrument so as not to be left out.

"I can't play anything," I said. "What instrument should I learn?"

"The trombone," said Niv, out of nowhere. It was so funny, because he'd not said a word all evening and here he was suggesting I learn the trombone. Everybody fell about laughing. Of course I was still laughing long after everyone else stopped.

"The triangle?" suggested Cat.

"How about the tambourine?" added JJ.

"Not the tambourine," said Dan, "she's not the type. She should play the harmonica. We could use a harmonica player."

"OK," I said, "I'm going to learn the harmonica!"

I have to admit here that up to this point in my life I've shown no musical ability whatsoever. I can't sing, and I've never been able to play anything in tune.

But, hey, why should that stop me?

After rehearsal, JJ offered to walk me home, as he was going to see his latest girlfriend, who lives in the same direction.

"So," I said, as casually as I could, "you know David Matthieson. . ."

JJ looked at me and grinned. He's far too sharp. I should have known he'd immediately work it out.

"My dad's his mum's cousin," he said, "so we're actually second cousins. He's all right. He's a really good lyricist. Dan's written a couple of our songs with him."

"Cat told me," I said, "about the songs."

"So, you like him?" asked JJ, his eyes twinkling. I blushed to the roots of my hair. This was so embarrassing.

"Don't tell him," I said, "please."

"What's it worth?" joked JJ.

"Well, it means I won't have to kill you," I said.

"All right," said JJ, putting his finger to his lips, "I won't say a word. It's funny, though. I sort of thought Cat and David were together. I got that one wrong."

I went to sleep that night worrying about what JJ had said. He'd thought they were an item. So it wasn't just me who thought there was something between them.

I wondered how many more people were going to find out about my liking David Matthieson. Gemma, Cat, Taylor and now JJ were all aware of my crush. I might as well just post it on Facebook.

At least, I thought, Tania Hamilton doesn't know. That would be awful.

The next day, at lunchtime, I found Dad cooking in a reasonably tidy kitchen. This was getting way too surreal. I checked under the sofa cushions and there was no kitchenware, which I took to be a good sign.

"So who's coming round?" I asked, watching Dad peeling carrots.

"Nobody," he replied.

"Then why are you cooking?" I was puzzled.

"Because that's what civilized people do on a Sunday," said Dad, opening the oven door. A delicious roast chicken smell filled the kitchen.

I went upstairs and did a double take as I passed the bathroom door. There was Ryan, wearing rubber gloves and clutching a bottle of toilet cleaner in one hand while holding the toilet brush in the other. He didn't notice me, so I crept to my room, to avoid him trying to hand over the task.

I lay down on my bed, staring at the ceiling, wondering if this was some sort of very realistic dream. Surely I would wake up and find Dad and Ryan back to their normal selves.

But it was not a dream. We sat around the table and had Sunday lunch together. OK, so there was zero conversation, just the sound of greedy munching, but you can't have everything. I nearly offered to wash up, then remembered Mum's warning, so instead said, "I'll help clear up," and we all did it together.

After lunch, I went down to the stables to break the news to Sheila that I couldn't help next weekend. I found her limping around the yard, looking grumpy, which I suppose was understandable. I'd be grumpy, I thought, with a big plaster cast on my leg.

"What do you do at a festival, then?" she asked, as if she'd never heard of them before. Which seemed pretty rich, seeing as her generation invented them.

"It's music, mostly. People go to see bands," I said, knowing that what I was saying was perfectly reasonable, but feeling that it sounded lame when I said it to Sheila with her beady eyes fixed on me.

"You look different," commented Sheila.

I was in my skinny black jeans and a pair of ankle boots, teamed with a purple T-shirt with a silver skull on it . . . and I was still wearing my black nail varnish. Not to mention black eyeliner and a little mascara. Normally when I saw Sheila I was make-up free and dressed in my tatty mucking-out clothes. So I suppose I looked pretty different.

"What's wrong with what I'm wearing?" I asked, feeling defensive.

"Nothing," said Sheila, "except you don't look like yourself. You look like somebody else."

Sheila is very straightforward and tells it like it is, but today I wasn't in the mood. I felt somehow judged, even though I'm sure she wasn't judging me at all.

"I'd better go," I said abruptly.

"Cup of tea?" Sheila suggested.

"No, thanks." I turned and walked away. After her comment, I wasn't in the mood to chat.

As I cycled home I thought how ridiculous it was that I was bothered about what Sheila thought about my image. Probably if she thought something looked wrong, it was a good thing.

On Monday, at lunchtime, David Matthieson walked into the lunch hall and made straight for our table. I was really surprised, then remembered that he was banned from the library. Maybe Cat had spoken to him, as she'd promised she would. I could feel my face going pink as he approached.

"Hi," he said, "mind if I join you?"

I said it was fine and he sat down.

"Hello, Cat!" he said.

"Hi," said Cat casually.

"I know you from English," David said to Taylor. "I'm David."

Taylor gave me a knowing look. Honestly, can he not be subtle for one second?

David opened the paper bag he was holding. He pulled out a cheese salad sandwich, an apple and a drink.

"A healthy and hearty repast, brave sir!" said Taylor, who was halfway through a giant bag of crisps.

This was great, I thought to myself. David Matthieson joins us in the lunch hall and Taylor reverts to talking like an idiot. I kicked Taylor under the table and glared at him.

"I keep my lunch money," said David. "I'm saving up for a new keyboard."

"David's written some of the lyrics for Mr Bleaney's songs," I explained, then wanted to kick myself even harder than I'd kicked Taylor. Now David would know I was finding stuff out about him.

"Awesome!" said Taylor, genuinely impressed.

"Sam's brother Ryan is into music too," said Cat. "He plays guitar. You should meet him."

David Matthieson smiled. "Yeah," he said.

Cat was trying to help, I could see that. She was trying to find an excuse to get David to come to my house. But I noticed that his smile wasn't for me, it was for her. There was this connection. I could see it.

My heart sank a little. How ridiculous of me, I thought, to even consider that somebody could like me better than Cat.

"I've got to go," I said, standing up. "I've got some homework to finish."

"What homework?" called out Taylor, looking worried because he's in a lot of my classes. But I was gone. I hurried out of the canteen, down the corridor and into the girls' toilets, where I sat in a cubicle and let two fat tears run down my cheeks.

This is not me at all. I don't normally feel sorry for myself. As I mopped at my eyes with loo paper, I decided that I was being completely ridiculous. I'd have to stop this immediately.

When the bell rang, I slipped out of the toilets and headed for the chemistry lab, only to run into David Matthieson. Talk about atrocious timing.

"Are you OK?" he said. Then he looked at me more closely and saw the telltale attractive blotchy redness around my eyes. "Have you been *crying*?"

"I'm fine now," I said.

"It's all right to cry," he said. "After all, your mum's walked out."

He patted me on the shoulder, then put his arm around me and squeezed me in a half hug. I thought that I might actually faint.

"Have you spoken to the school counsellor?" he asked.

"I'll think about it," I said. I started to walk towards the science lab, and he walked with me, although his lesson was, I was pretty sure, in the opposite direction. Outside the chemistry lab, he asked again if I was sure I was OK.

"Thanks," I said. "Honestly, I'll be fine."

"You can talk to me about it any time," he said, giving me an intense look. He disappeared off down the corridor.

When I walked into the lab, my face was all flushed. Darcie was already setting up the experiment. It involved

153

test tubes, some blue crystals and a beaker of some clear liquid.

"What's happened to you?" asked Darcie.

"I don't know," I said. I could still feel his arm around me. I could still feel the way he'd looked at me.

"You *don't know* what's just happened to you?" Darcie looked at me dubiously.

I shook my head.

Darcie handed me a pair of goggles.

"Well, at least try to look as if you're helping me with this experiment," she said. "Honestly, Sam, recently I don't know what's got into you!"

MY STATUS
Sam Wallis
Likes the paintings of **Eileen Malloy**.
Penny Griffiths Looked at her website, very interesting. Unfortunately her paintings would clash with our three-piece suite and curtains, which are peach coloured.
Sam Wallis Never mind, Auntie P.
Darcie Clelland Is the artist Cat's mum?
Sam Wallis Yes.
Hanna Kermack I love these paintings!
Gemma Smith Me too.
Tania Hamilton They are rubbish.
Angela Murray I agree, they're really lame.

Chapter Thirteen

Every lunchtime that week, David came and sat with me and Cat and Taylor. Cat – in matchmaking mode – kept saying things to make me sound great. Like "Sam's an excellent horse rider" or "Sam's on the athletics team, aren't you, Sam?"

David would nod politely, but – again – I was sure his warmest smiles were for Cat. Occasionally something would happen that would give me hope. Like when he went on again about liking pandas, and glanced over at me as if it meant something, our private joke.

But then David and Cat would reminisce about something they'd done together or with the band, and I'd feel completely left out and sure that their bond was something stronger and more meaningful than friendship, even if they didn't know it themselves.

In short, I was clueless as to what was going on. In the end I relaxed and managed to put to one side the fact that I had a massive crush on him. I began to think that Cat was right when she said that I should just be friends with him, and if anything else developed that would be a bonus. I actually began to be myself. We talked about music, and I mentioned, jokingly, that I was going to learn the harmonica.

"I've got an old harmonica you can have," said David. "I'll bring it in."

True to his word, he brought it in the very next day. I, of course, blushed beetroot when he handed it to me. I couldn't help thinking that if I played it and my lips were where his had been, it would almost be like kissing him.

How pathetic is that?

On Thursday lunchtime Hanna and Darcie joined us, and Taylor was on his best form ever, entertaining us all by reenacting his Puffy-Wheats act. I thought that Hanna might choke, she was laughing so much.

"So, are you going to go out with Ryan again?" I asked Cat innocently.

Cat shrugged. "We're all going to the festival, aren't we?" she said.

David, who I knew had heard what I said to Cat, didn't seem to react at all. There was no sign of surprise or jealousy. I wondered if I'd made it clear enough that they'd been on a date.

I must have, because Taylor clutched at his heart, acting all exaggeratedly broken-hearted.

"Tell me . . . *tell me* you're not seeing another man?" he pleaded with Cat.

"I'm afraid so," laughed Cat.

Taylor put his hand to his forehead. "I am destined to die alone!" he cried, so loud that it carried across the lunch hall.

We all fell about laughing, he was so comical. I looked over to see Tania looking the angriest I've ever seen her. She couldn't bear to see a group of people having fun, and it being nothing to do with her.

That night, I got another message from Gemma, who was getting very excited.

Gemma Smith
In just under two days, boats will arrive ... and off them will step hundreds of people, including lots and lots of boys!! Shona and Elaine have dropped the burgundy look and have dyed their hair blonde, and Shona bought a pair of false eyelashes. I am not convinced about them. It looks as if she has two giant spiders camping out under her eyebrows, so I've decided to give that look a miss, although I've been applying "lash builder" mascara and think I've perfected my technique.

There are six marching bands coming along. Apparently they line up and take turns marching around the showground competing in different ways, such as how good they are as a band, their marching skills and how smartly dressed they are. I'm sure this was very interesting in the days before television.

The part I'm looking forward to most is the beach

party in the evening. Apparently it can get quite wild. Mum and Dad do not know about the "wild" part, and think that I will be safe in the company of Shona and Elaine, because all they've ever seen them do is knit. If only they knew. Hee hee.

Sam Wallis
The beach party sounds immense. I hope it goes fantastically.

I'm staying with Cat tomorrow night and then we get a bus with the band (how great is THAT?) to the festival. The only downside is that Ryan will be there (boo!). I am sharing a two-man tent with Cat. I will probably snore like a rhinoceros and everyone at the festival will hear me.

By the way, you know LOML? Well, Cat's been doing her best on my behalf, but suspect he likes her, not me. Let's face it, the only proper attention I've had from him is sympathy. But I'm not going to feel sorry for myself. After all, I've got the festival to look forward to.

WHY have you changed your Facebook profile picture to a picture of a Highland cow? Are you finally losing it?

Gemma Smith
I lost it a long, long time ago, babes.

Very sorry if LOYL likes Cat. Promise you won't let it get you down. Get out there and forget him.

I'm feeling sorry for Cat already because yes, you DO snore. Not like a rhinoceros ... you sound more like a water buffalo.

Sam Wallis

Cheers for that, that's a real confidence booster!!

As far as LOML is concerned, I promise I am fine about it. Lots of cod, halibut, and various other types of fish in the sea.

Gemma Smith

Glad to hear you are over LOYL. Have knitted loads of scarves to try to sell. With that, and going along with her goat's cheese enterprise, I am so much in Mum's good books, I might ask her if I can stay with you when we're all back in the summer.

Sam Wallis

I can't wait to see you. I need to hear first-hand all about what you get up to.

GOOD LUCK for the weekend. Got to go now and do nail varnish.

Gemma Smith

Enjoy the festival. Speak to you soon. Try not to embarrass yourself too much!!!!

I couldn't believe her cheek. "Try not to embarrass yourself too much" indeed. I'd just have to prove to her, and myself, that I can be extremely mature. Like Cat.

It was hard to concentrate at school on Friday. All I could think about was that I was having a sleepover at Cat's house and then, early on Saturday, we were off to the festival. I rushed home from school to pack my stuff.

I was just getting ready to leave for Cat's house when the phone call came. Dad took it, and initially seemed pleased that it was Mum.

"Hello, Julie!" he said. "Where are you, then? When are you flying back?"

Then his face changed, and it became clear that all was not well.

"An extra *week*?" Dad spluttered. "How do you think you're going to get the annual leave to do that?"

Looking extremely angry, Dad took the phone off into the kitchen, no doubt so we wouldn't hear him shouting at her.

After five minutes he walked back into the living room, still talking into the phone. He no longer looked angry. He looked worried.

"I see," he said. "That's very kind of them. . . No, it's fine by us if it's what you want."

I wondered why he was suddenly talking so reasonably.

"We miss you," he said, finally, "me, Sam and Ryan. We all miss you very much. Love you."

He hung up the phone and sat down on the sofa. He put

his head in his hands.

"Dad, what's going on?" I asked. Even Ryan looked worried.

Dad rubbed his hands over his face, then looked up and made an attempt at a smile.

"Your mum's not coming home this weekend," he said. "They're staying on another week, they got some deal. . ."

I felt worried. Why was she jumping at the chance to stay away from us? Maybe there really was something wrong with Mum and Dad's marriage.

"Why's she doing this?" asked Ryan, indignant.

"Your mum's not been well," said Dad. "It was all those extra shifts and long hours they pushed her into. It turns out she's been signed off work for a month with *stress*. And this is the first I hear of it!"

Dad looked quite upset. "I should have paid more attention," he said. "I knew things were getting on top of her. I'd no idea how much."

"Do you want me to stay?" I asked. It seemed wrong to leave him like this.

"No, you go and enjoy yourselves," he said. "Don't you worry about me. I'm all right."

"I'm sure she'll feel better after her holiday," I said, patting him on the shoulder. "It's only one more week."

At least Ryan wasn't leaving till the morning, I thought, as I cycled to Cat's house. I felt sorry for Dad. He'd looked so disappointed when he realized Mum wasn't coming home yet, and gutted to realize he hadn't noticed how bad

161

her stress was. This was not the exuberant, loud and cheery Dad I was used to.

MY STATUS
Sam Wallis
Hopes Gemma enjoys the weekend (!!!!)
Gemma Smith You too!
Tania Hamilton Hope I don't bump into panda features at the Plastic Moon Festival.

Chapter Fourteen

I checked my messages on Facebook at Cat's house and saw the comment from Tania. She'd been making little digs at me for weeks, but this one seemed to cross the line. I showed it to Cat.

"That's *mean*," she said.

"Well," I said, "we'll just have to ignore her, won't we?"

At nine, the minibus arrived, driven by JJ's dad, who was a jolly "joker" type, eerily similar to my dad. I found myself wedged between JJ and a silent Niv.

"First festival?" asked JJ. Really, I wondered, did I have it written on my forehead or something? I had hoped it was not so obvious.

"Yeah," I said, trying to sound casual.

"Have you told her about the compost toilets?" asked Dan.

I looked round at them, trying to work out if this was a wind-up.

"You are joking, right?" I said.

"I'm afraid not," chipped in Cat's mum. "The Plastic Moon Festival is an eco-festival. But don't worry. They're fine once you get used to them."

"Once you get used to the *smell*!" laughed Dan.

Suddenly, I was not so sure about all of this. Nobody had mentioned the compost toilets. What else did I not know about?

Niv didn't say anything. It was JJ who chatted about the band, and his family. We were able to compare notes on having dads who liked to be the life and soul of the party. He also had some funny stories about girls he went out with, and he seemed to have been out with lots, which I wasn't surprised about, because he did seem to have such an easy charm about him.

"I can't help myself!" he said, when Cat told him off for his exploits. "I'm just not a one-woman man!"

After an hour we stopped at a service station. I'd given Cat my ticket money, but I still had loads left out of the huge amount of cash Mum left in my sock drawer, so I treated myself to a giant bar of chocolate, an apple (to be healthy), crisps and a can of Coke. Back on the bus, JJ and Niv both kept asking for chocolate and crisps, which saved me from making a complete pig of myself.

Niv must have decided I was all right due to my sharing my food with him, because he actually spoke to me after that. Here I was, on a bus with a real band, on my way to a real festival, talking to an eighteen-year-old with tattoos. I wished that Gemma could see me.

Cat's mum was up at the front, reading a newspaper and chatting with JJ's dad. Ryan was deep in conversation with Cat, as he had been for the entire journey so far. I realized that Ryan had said more to Cat in the last hour than he'd probably said to his entire family in a year.

The countryside rushed past, and after another hour we were there. I pressed my nose against the window as we passed hordes of people, all wearing wellies despite it being warmish and sunny, due to the inevitable "festival mud". I was glad I'd brought mine, but not so glad that they were bright yellow with green spots on them, because of course they clashed with my new, more mature image.

We left the minibus at the car park and trudged to another field, where we pitched our tents. Or, rather, Cat and her mum pitched Cat's and my tent while I watched in admiration. It seemed to just ping up by itself and then they hammered in a couple of pegs and it was done. This camping lark, I decided, wasn't so bad really. It looked easy.

"I think I'll explore," I said.

"OK," Cat's mum said vaguely, as she poured hot water into tin mugs with teabags in them, "have fun!"

While I was exploring and getting my bearings about what was where, I was scanning the thousands of faces I passed, just in case I spotted David Matthieson. I knew it was like looking for a needle in a haystack, and it was pointless anyway because I suspected he liked Cat, but I couldn't help myself.

There were people in jester's hats, and people wearing flowers in their hair. There were Morris dancers and jugglers and fire-eaters and stilt-walkers. There were dancers in multicoloured wigs, and human statues spray-painted silver, and a crowd of girls all dressed as fairies. There were loads of ordinary people too, forming queues at food stalls, or walking around like me, taking it all in. But among all of those hordes there was no sign of him, and I was annoyed with myself for even looking.

I saw where the main stage was, where the top bands would be playing. It was quite big. I knew Mr Bleaney were playing in what was called the "New Talent" tent, which was for new young bands who wanted to get spotted. They would not draw huge crowds, Cat had told me, but at least it was a start. While they'd played lots of local gigs, this was their first big festival, so they were pretty nervous.

Checking the programme of events, which was on the other side of the site map, I saw that they were playing at nine-thirty p.m., which was good. The crowds would be warmed up by then. Also, the band on the main stage then was not the type of band to attract the same sort of people who'd like Mr Bleaney.

After another half hour of walking about, some candyfloss, and some phone checking, I made my way back to our field. I was busy congratulating myself on my ace navigational skills when I saw, from a distance, David

Matthieson. He was sitting with Cat and her mum, having a cup of tea!

I couldn't believe it. I'd been out for almost an hour, all round the site looking for him, and he was *here*! I sauntered up as casually as I could.

"Hi," I said.

They all looked up, startled. They had been so deep in conversation they'd not noticed me approaching.

"Hello, Sam!" said David. "I like your wellies, very . . . colourful. I'm glad I brought my sunglasses."

He grinned, and I couldn't help smiling back.

"Want a cup of tea?" asked Cat.

"No, thanks," I said, "I just popped back to get my camera. I'm going to go and check out the sculpture field."

This was not true. I'd not come back for my camera, and I'd not been going to see the sculpture field. But I couldn't bear to stay there, with him talking to Cat.

"Can I come?" asked David.

This threw me. I'd assumed he'd want to stay with her.

"Oh, OK," I said, trying to sound casual about it, instead of madly enthusiastic, which is what I was feeling inside.

I looked at Cat. "Are you coming?" I asked.

"No," she said, smiling at me meaningfully, "you have fun!"

I thought what a good friend she was. She was willing to stay and chat to her mum so that I could have a chance with David Matthieson. I knew she'd rather be coming along.

We walked in silence to the sculpture field. I kept thinking up things to say, but they all sounded lame. I didn't want to give away how inexperienced I was about this whole festival business.

Then I wondered if this qualified as an actual date. David had asked if he could come along in quite a casual way, but then again he hadn't needed to come at all. He could have stayed with Cat. The question was, was he attracted by the idea of the sculptures, or by the idea of being with me? From our lunchtime conversations, I knew he liked art and was even thinking about going to art school. So maybe it was the sculptures after all.

I decided that I'd treat it as a date, just to be on the safe side. Otherwise I might miss an important opportunity. I had to be on the alert for signals so that I could react appropriately.

I read somewhere that ninety per cent of communication is nonverbal. Apparently you can tell if someone has a rapport with you by whether or not their feet point towards you. I decided to look out for that. And I made sure that at every opportunity my feet, clad in my yellow wellies with the green spots on them, pointed towards him. Which at times made me walk in a slightly odd manner.

This not knowing if I was on a date or not business was most confusing.

POSITIVES

* I can still be optimistic. There's still hope.
* I can use it as a chance to practise for when I'm on a proper, official date.

NEGATIVES

* Danger that I might behave inappropriately. And look like an idiot.

The sculpture field was amazing. One corner was stone sculptures brought all the way from Africa.

My favourite sculpture was one of a mother holding a baby where the arms went all the way round in a circle, and the mother's head was bowed down.

"I LOVE that one!" I said, enthusiastically, pointing at it. Then, as soon as I'd said it, I regretted it. My pointing it out could, I realized, make him think that I was desperate to have his baby. I blushed bright red at the thought.

"It's great," he agreed. "I think it's one of the best ones too."

There was a section called "Creative Corner" where you could make your own sculptures out of large lumps of clay. The finished sculptures were displayed on rows of tables along the back.

"Do you want to have a go?" asked David. I could see that he wanted to.

"OK," I said.

Luckily they gave us aprons. I was relieved because I didn't want to get red clay on my black clothes.

He immediately started to knead and shape his clay as if he knew exactly what he was doing.

"Do you like sculptures then?" I asked.

"Yeah, I love 3D stuff," said David. "Cat hates art, did you know that?"

"No," I said, wishing he wouldn't talk about Cat.

"It's because of her mum's painting," he said. "She said she could never be as good as her mum, so she never tried."

"Well, at least she's got her music," I said.

I looked at the lump of clay I'd been given, wondering what on earth I could make.

I thought of trying to do a sculpture of Scuzzball, and started going to work. I tried to show him sleeping, curled up in a ball with his tail stretching round. Then I shaped his little triangular head and pointy ears.

"Look, Mummy," said a boy who was walking past, "that girl's doing Yoda from *Star Wars*!"

I squidged the clay up again, glancing over at David. He was doing a fantastic sculpture of a winter tree. It was fascinating to watch him at work, fashioning the roots and branches, pulling out pieces of clay into smaller and smaller strands as the branches got finer. As I watched, I idly rolled my clay in my hands, forgetting I was supposed to be sculpting as well.

"Wow! That's so great!" I said, watching as the tree got

more twisted. "It's like one of the trees in *Harry Potter*."

The artist who was running the Creative Corner came round. She was the most outrageous hippy, with long dreadlocks to her waist and tie-dyed dungarees beneath an enormous jumper that looked like it had been knitted from dog hair. She was very impressed with David's tree, going on about beauty and natural form.

"And what are *you* doing?" she asked me. I held up my lump of clay with a smile, about to say that I'd been so busy watching David that I'd not got round to doing anything.

"Astonishing!" she said, breathlessly. "Do you mind?"

She took my lump of clay from me with reverence, as if it was some sort of holy relic. Then she held it up in the air. Basically it was just a lump of clay that I'd been rolling between my hands so now it was sort of egg shaped.

"I hope we can show it?" she said. "What would you like to give it as a title?"

I looked at the vaguely egg-shaped piece of clay.

"Egg," I said.

"Of course!" she enthused. "Perfect!"

David's tree was also put on display, and as the artist went on about my "innate talent", I felt very proud of myself, even if it had all been totally accidental.

When we were taking off our aprons, there was an awkward moment. I was struggling to get mine over my head, so he reached over to help me. This meant that his face was close to mine.

Our faces inches apart, I noticed him looking down at my mouth. This, I was sure beyond any doubt, was a signal that he wanted to kiss me. I closed my eyes and slightly pouted. Then I felt his hand wiping my chin.

"You've got some clay on your face," he explained, looking at me oddly as I reopened my eyes and stopped pouting.

"Oh, thanks," I said. Why, why, WHY, I thought, was I such an idiot? Of *course* he wasn't intending to kiss me. Why on earth would he?

"Are you looking forward to Mr Bleaney tonight?" he asked as we walked on.

I was glad that he was acting as if everything was normal and I hadn't just arranged my face as if expecting to be snogged.

"Yes," I said, "are you?"

"I'll be there," he said. "I hope they get noticed. I was wanting to ask. . ."

But he didn't get to finish his sentence because he was interrupted.

"I told you that David had a girlfriend, Mummy," said a bratty voice. "It's that smelly girl who had the cake all over her."

David's mum and his little sister Jessica were standing in front of us. Jessica was in a multicoloured stripy jumper with coloured braids in her curly hair. His mum was looking at me quizzically, no doubt wondering if her son had taken leave of his senses.

"David! You've got your phone on silent again!" said his mum in a slightly plaintive voice. I reckoned she was one of those long-suffering martyr types.

"Mum, Jessica, this is Sam," said David. "Sam, this is my mum and this is my *very naughty* little sister!"

He reached over and tickled Jessica, who shrieked and squirmed away from him, giggling.

"There's a problem with the tent," complained his mum. "The zip keeps sticking. I wonder if you could come and have a look at it?"

He sighed and shrugged his shoulders at me in a *what can I do?* sort of a way. I felt sorry for him.

"No probs," he said good-naturedly. "See you later, Sam!"

They walked off, David taking his little sister's hand and swinging it as they walked.

MY STATUS
Sam Wallis
Is at the Plastic Moon Festival and has just eaten some candyfloss.
Tania Hamilton How old are you again?
Sam Wallis You can never be too old for candyfloss.
Gemma Smith I hope I'm eating candyfloss when I'm a hundred.
Tania Hamilton It's probably all you'll be able to eat, you'll only have one tooth.

Chapter Fifteen

"Did you like the sculptures?" asked Cat's mum, from a camping chair. She was curled up, reading a book.

"They were great, you should see them," I said.

"Cat's gone there," said Cat's mum. "I think she was hoping to catch up with you. You should give her a call and meet up. Between you and me, I think she's nervous about tonight. You could help her take her mind off things."

I rang Cat and it turned out she was at the food stalls, looking for something to eat for lunch. Realizing that I was actually quite hungry, I raced off to join her.

She was standing beside the all-day breakfast van, finishing a bacon roll. They smelled so outrageously good that I ordered one, smothering it in tomato ketchup. We strolled off, taking in the outlandish sights. We got to the street performance area and wondered why suddenly everybody was looking at us and laughing. They seemed to be looking behind us.

We turned round. A man in a bowler hat and suit was standing whistling nonchalantly. We carried on, everybody laughing again. We stopped and turned round; there he was again. We carried on and this time I looked round and caught him. He was following us, imitating our walks and miming my eating the bacon roll. It was quite funny and I laughed, but I really felt embarrassed. I looked to see how Cat was reacting and as I expected, she was completely cool about it, just giving a wry smile.

We'd only just escaped the evil mime artist when who should appear out of nowhere in the crowd not far away? You've guessed it. David Matthieson, his mother and his sister. Of course. This was getting ridiculous. Here was I holding a giant half-eaten bacon roll and they had to walk up at that exact moment.

"Hello there!" David said. "Having a snack?"

Suddenly the comedy of the situation hit me. Cat had finished her roll, so it was me he saw holding the bacon roll, with animal fat practically dripping down my chin.

I couldn't help it. I started to giggle. Which turned into a laugh, over which I, of course, had absolutely no control.

"Are you OK?" said David's mum, as if she thought I might be ill. I couldn't reply, I was laughing so much.

"It's nice to see you, Cat," she continued. "How are you?"

"Very well, thanks, Mrs Matthieson," said Cat.

I carried on laughing. David was looking at me oddly.

"You must be excited about tonight," David's mum continued.

I couldn't stop. Tears were rolling down my cheeks.

"Yes, and a bit nervous," said Cat.

"Are you sure you're OK?" said David, smiling and shaking his head as I nodded to him that I was fine.

"Lovely to see you again, Cat," said David's mum. "Good luck!"

"We've got to go," said David. "See you later!"

I tried to weigh up the positives and negatives of my bacon-roll-eating incident.

POSITIVES

* I can now stop pretending to be a vegetarian. A huge relief.

NEGATIVES

* David Matthieson now thinks I'm an evil flesh-eating murderer.
* He probably thought I was laughing an evil flesh-eating murdering laugh.

Cat looked at me after they'd gone and shook her head. She didn't need to say anything. I was still laughing a sort of hopeless, hysterical laugh of despair. We walked on, passing the mime artist again. He followed us again, mimicking my mad laughter. Which showed me exactly how stupid I looked.

MY STATUS
Sam Wallis
Is looking forward to seeing **Mr Bleaney** tonight.
Gemma Smith and **Hanna Kermack** like this.
Tania Hamilton Oh no! The panda's going to Mr Bleaney!!!!!

Chapter Sixteen

When Cat and I got back to camp, Ryan was waiting. He must have fallen asleep when he went in his tent, then woken up to find everybody was gone. Even Cat's mum had gone wandering. He looked fed up.

"Hey, Ryan!" said Cat. "Want to come and check out the wind chime field with me?"

"Yeah, that sounds *brilliant*!" said Ryan, who I happen to know thinks wind chimes are lame, because he's said so on more than one occasion. Honestly, I thought to myself bitterly, first he's off watching some film about a dying girl, now he's off to bask in the sound of wind chimes. Talk about losing all self-respect.

I curled up in Cat's mum's camping chair and picked up the book she was reading. It was about the life of Van Gogh. Which was pretty tragic, what with nobody buying his paintings and him getting thrown out of cafes. No wonder he cut off his ear.

Being a mad artist getting no recognition would have to

be tough, I decided. I tried to imagine the good and bad aspects of being Van Gogh.

POSITIVES

* Painting masterpieces and having deep, genius thoughts.

NEGATIVES

* Being poor and having to beg for food.
* Being mad.
* Losing your ear.
* Everyone thinking you're rubbish.

After a while Cat returned with Ryan, who looked exactly like someone who'd endured wind chimes for the sake of love.

Dan wandered up, playing his guitar as he walked and looking like an underfed, slightly vampire-like minstrel. Then JJ arrived with Niv in tow. People came and went all afternoon.

There was a definite atmosphere of expectation. None of the band could sit still, and for the next few hours they got increasingly wound up, pacing around as their nervous energy built up. Although they weren't performing till nine-thirty, they had to go up earlier for set-up and to use the rehearsal tent. Ryan went with them, to help out, he said. I decided I'd only get in their way so I'd wait until later.

After they left, I hung about with Cat's mum for a while, then – feeling bored – decided to go for another explore.

I saw Tania's post yet again comparing me to a panda. I couldn't believe she kept going on and on about it. I wished she wasn't at the festival and wasn't going to be at the gig. Why, I wondered, couldn't she just be pleasant now and again? I closed my eyes and concentrated very hard until I had a clear image in my head of Tania being pursued through the wind chimes field by a determined goat with fangs. I felt slightly better.

I decided not to go to the children's play area in case David Matthieson thought that I was stalking him. Instead I did another round of the food stalls, getting myself a very nice sort of chicken wrap thing with all sorts of toppings. I was sure the Emperor of Meat would not approve of the quality of the chicken, which made it all the more delicious.

As I munched and walked around people-watching, I wondered what Gemma was doing. Had she sold her scarves yet? Were there any fit boys for her to chase? I was surprised she hadn't replied to a message I'd sent an hour earlier which said "How's it going?" But then again, phone reception was patchy on her island, so there was every chance she wouldn't get it till tomorrow.

There were some fire-eaters and jugglers putting on a show so I joined the crowd watching, as it was pretty spectacular. One of the fire-eaters stopped to have a drink of water and winked at me! He was quite cute, if slightly covered in soot. He had dark hair and sea-green eyes with dark eyelashes, and he looked sort of mischievous. I reckoned he had to be at least sixteen, maybe even seventeen.

I, of course, blushed to the roots of my hair. When the show was over he strolled over.

"Hi, I'm Jake," he said. "Did you like the show?"

"It was great," I said. "But how do you learn to eat fire? I mean, it's not something they teach you at school."

Jake laughed. "I suppose not. I learned from my dad. We've been doing all the festivals ever since I can remember. We've got our own act now, me and my brothers."

He pointed at the three other boys, who did look like his brothers, now that I thought about it.

"Well, you're really good," I said. I couldn't think of anything else to say so I went red again and then said "Bye!" and walked away.

"What's your name?" he called after me.

I turned round. "Sam!" I called.

"See you around, Sam," he called back.

His attention gave me a boost, after all my insecurities of wondering about David's feelings for Cat. And he did have fantastic eyes.

I couldn't help wondering what it would be like to go out with a fire-eater.

POSITIVES
* A convenient way to toast marshmallows.

NEGATIVES
* Charred, numb lips (theirs) could hamper kissing.
* They might accidentally set you on fire.

The whole being sort-of-chatted-up by a fire-eater incident got me so worked up (as it's not often that older boys pay any attention to me), I had to go and get a milkshake to calm myself down. Then I checked my phone yet again. I got a signal and was excited, hoping there'd be a message from Gems. But there wasn't. I did a quick post and then had another wander around.

I went back to the campsite and changed. Everybody else had gone. I put on some make-up, making sure I didn't overdo the eyeliner after Tania's recent jibes. There was nobody to ask if I looked good or not, but I was pretty sure I looked OK.

I stuck the rest of the money I got from mum – and there was still plenty left – in the pocket of my jeans, and then I was ready to go. It felt weird going down all on my own. This was the first big night out since

Gemma left and it was so wrong to not have her with me.

MY STATUS
Sam Wallis
Did a sculpture that looked like an egg, watched some fire-eaters and had a milkshake. Now off to see **Mr Bleaney**.
Tania Hamilton Tragic, tragic and tragic. Remember to wear lots of eyeliner, it suits you SO MUCH.

Chapter Seventeen

I got down to the gig half an hour before Mr Bleaney was due to go on. I saw Cat to the side of the stage, looking quite pale and nervous. I caught her eye and made sure I gave her a huge thumbs up. Then I saw Cat's mum. The only trouble was that in order to get to her, I had to walk past Tania and Angela.

"It's the candyfloss-eating panda!" said Tania. I smiled like I thought it was a great joke. Which it wasn't. It wasn't the sort of fun banter between friends that I'd have with Gemma. With Tania it was different; it was meant to hurt. She knew it, and I knew it.

"I like your scarf," said Angela, but in a sort of sarcastic voice which made me wonder if she meant it. I suddenly really missed Gemma. It would be good to have her by my side right now, I thought. We'd exchange glances about Tania and Angela's little game and somehow it wouldn't matter any more.

"Can your friend sing?" asked Tania. "Or did they just

hire her because she looks good?"

"She's good," I replied.

"Well, hasn't she just got it all," said Tania, in a sarcastic way.

"I like the drummer," said Angela.

"The bass player and the lead guitarist . . . they're total freaks," decided Tania. "But that's OK cos they're musicians, so they're not complete losers."

"Tania, you do say the weirdest things," I said.

I don't think Tania liked that, because she glared at me. But I didn't care.

"Got to go," I said, and walked on.

I was just trying to push through the crowd to get to Cat's mum when David appeared by my side.

"Hi," he said, "would you like something to drink?"

My stomach gave a little flip, just because he was standing close to me.

"Thanks, I'll have an orange juice, please," I managed. He disappeared off to the bar.

As I stood waiting for him, Tania and Angela came over. I wished they would leave me alone.

"Are you seeing him?" Angela asked.

"No," I said. "We're just friends."

"Figures," said Tania. "He's probably in love with Cat and just using you to get close to her."

David came back with my orange juice and I was glad of the chance to walk away from Tania and Angela. He seemed happy to be out on his own and free of his babysitting duties. We moved through the crowd, but I could no longer see Cat's mum, so we stopped and stood together, waiting for the band to come on.

"Mum's OK," he said, "but she's always got something for me to do, or she's asking me to watch Jessica for her. I'm glad I've finally escaped!"

I couldn't help myself as I looked at him talk. I wondered what it would be like to kiss him. *Stop it!* I told myself, and tried to focus on what he was saying.

Mr Bleaney came onstage and the small crowd cheered and clapped, which turned the small crowd into a bigger crowd.

Cat looked very vulnerable all of a sudden, standing in the middle of the stage in front of the microphone. JJ played some opening drumbeats, Niv came in with the bass line and then Cat and Dan did their stuff.

They were incredible. More than incredible. They were a hundred times better than in the rehearsal I saw, where I thought they were amazing.

With every song, the crowd grew and the cheers got louder. Suddenly this unknown band playing in a side stage were getting a lot of attention. People were filming on their mobile phones, and others were coming from the main stage to see what all the commotion was about, or because friends had tweeted or texted to get over and see this band.

Cat looked much less unsure of herself with every song, and was now looking radiant. I could see her as a real star.

I looked across at Tania, and was pleased to see her

looking even more annoyed than she usually looked when Cat was getting attention. She'd probably been hoping Cat would be rubbish so she could tell everybody. But Cat was good; she was more than good.

Then Mr Bleaney sang "Looking for You", and as Cat's lovely voice soared and she sang about lost love, the crowd fell quiet.

I looked over at David and as he watched her, I saw something in his face. A really intense look.

So I was right. Despite all my false hopes along the way, I'd actually been right from my very first suspicions. You can't choose who you like, even if it's hopeless and you don't have a chance. This was true for me, and it was true – I could see – for David.

"I've got to go," I mouthed to him, and moved back in the crowd, blindly pushing my way past people to try to get out of the tent.

It came to the end of the song. The crowd went absolutely wild. Cheering, stamping, calling out for more.

I just needed to get out before I made a fool of myself in front of everybody. I managed to find my way past all of the people, and started to run as fast as I could back towards the campsite.

I wasn't looking where I was going, and the beginnings of tears were blurring my vision, which is why I ran right into Jake, the fire-eater.

"Whoa! Are you OK?" he said, catching me by the

shoulders.

"Yeah, I'm fine," I lied, "I just need to get back to my tent."

"I'm surprised to see you running out of there," he said. "Everybody else is desperate to get in. Who's playing?"

"Just a band my friend's in; it's called Mr Bleaney," I explained.

He looked impressed. "Listen, I'm meeting some people," he said. "Want to come along?"

I was surprised he was asking me. I wondered if he was assuming I was older than I was because I said my friend was in Mr Bleaney.

I thought about the alternative, sitting alone in my tent and then having to see David and Cat coming back with the others. Having to face up to the fact that even though she wasn't interested in him, he was in love with her. I looked at Jake, who gave me a cheeky grin. He seemed OK. A friendly sort of a person. I decided there was no harm in it.

"What would you like?" he asked, at the bar in the giant drinks marquee.

"Just an orange juice," I said.

"Coming right up," he said, smiling.

Being introduced to Jake's friends, who all looked sixteen or seventeen, felt weird, because they were treating me like an equal, not like someone who was younger. I didn't feel intimidated; having been hanging round with

Mr Bleaney for the last day gave me some confidence. In fact, I even managed to drop their name into the conversation.

"Wow! You know Mr Bleaney!" said one girl. "They are, like, SO COOL! I really like the drummer."

Jake and his friends were great fun, and he paid me a lot of attention. He bought me another orange juice, but it tasted a bit strange. Maybe it hadn't been in the fridge or something. We were at a festival after all.

I suppose I was flattered Jake seemed so interested in me. And it took my mind off how gutted I was feeling about David liking Cat.

I suddenly felt light-headed, and decided to get some fresh air. I wondered if it was because the tent was overcrowded.

"I'm going to the loo," I lied. Then when I got outside, I gulped in the fresh air as if it were a refreshing drink of water. I walked about for five minutes, and soon began to feel much better.

When I got back I was OK for a while but then began to feel extremely weird. The room began to sway, as if the floor was tipping to one side. People's voices sounded quite far away. I leaned against Jake, who put his arm around me.

Around us people began to talk about going back to their tents for a party.

"You coming?" said Jake, from what sounded like the other side of the marquee, although he was right beside me.

"Got to get back," I whispered in his ear. His ear suddenly looked very strange. Not like an ear at all.

"What did she say? Is she OK?" asked one of his brothers.

"She's coming back with us," I heard him say. Which I thought was odd, as I'd just told him the opposite.

"No," I said.

Jake put his arm around me and led me out of the marquee, following the group back to where their tents were pitched. I kept trying to tell him I wanted to go back to my own tent, but he didn't seem to hear. It was like he was frogmarching me along, but I was feeling so dizzy I couldn't resist.

What was wrong with me?

There was a campfire, I remember. There was singing. I was sitting on the ground leaning against Jake but I couldn't seem to move. I was feeling so dizzy and nauseous I knew that there was something very, very wrong with me.

This was all wrong. I didn't even know him. I wondered if he was going to try to kiss me, and knew if he did I probably wouldn't be able to stop him. I'd never been kissed before. I didn't want my first kiss to be like this.

"Excuse me," said a voice above us, "do you know she's only thirteen?"

Jake looked up. "Whoa!" he said. "Thirteen! No, I didn't know, mate, trust me!"

"Sam! Are you all right, Sam?" the voice sounded concerned. I couldn't even focus on who was there.

"She's practically unconscious," said the voice of a girl accusingly. "Did you do the old vodka trick again? Nice one, Jake."

"I can't help it if she's underage, I didn't know!" I heard him say indignantly.

I was lifted up by two people. I'd no idea who they were. Then I was half carried, half dragged for a while, and during that time sometimes I was awake and sometimes I wasn't.

It was the coffee that made me come round. Hot coffee tipped into my mouth. I spluttered, gasped and then I was very, very sick on myself and on the ground.

"She's OK," said Cat's voice, sounding relieved.

"Are you all right, Sam?" said Cat's mum. I opened my eyes and checked that it was her and this was not a dream.

"I feel so ill," I said. "I want to die."

STATUS
Tania Hamilton
Can't believe **Sam Wallis** last night.
Becky Robinson Wot happened?
Tania Hamilton MAJOR embarrassment. Carried back to her tent being sick down herself!!!!!!!!
Becky Robinson Wot????
Tania Hamilton Got in a right state. Take the shame, Sam.

Taylor Griffen No way!

Tania Hamilton She is grounded <u>for ever</u>.

Hanna Kermack Poor Sam. Hope she's all right.

Tania Hamilton She doesn't deserve your pity, believe me.

Chapter Eighteen

When I woke up in the morning, I was in a sleeping bag in my pyjamas. My head hurt worse than it's ever hurt in my entire life. I supposed this was what people called a hangover.

After a while I got the strength to crawl out of the tent. Cat's mum was sitting outside; there was nobody else there. It felt like late morning.

"Hello," I said, which sounded pathetic.

"How are you feeling?" she asked. She looked upset and tired, as if she'd not slept well.

"Terrible," I replied. "I'm so sorry. I'm really, really sorry."

She didn't reply, which was worse. She just sat looking disappointed and let down.

"Where is everybody?" I asked.

"They've gone to see a band," she said, "but when they get back, we're leaving early. JJ's dad's coming to pick us up."

"Because of me?"

"Yes."

Silence. I felt full of shame.

"What made you do it?" she asked. "You're only *thirteen*, for God's sake! How could you go off with a total stranger and get drunk? Do you have *any idea* what danger you put yourself in? Do you know how harmful alcohol is?"

"I didn't get drunk," I protested, "I was drinking orange juice. I think he must have spiked it. A girl said something about the vodka trick."

Cat's mum looked as if she was deciding whether or not to believe me. "That's a very serious accusation, Sam."

"It's true, I was drinking orange juice. It *must* have been spiked."

She thought for a while. Then she spoke. "Can you hurry and get dressed? We know where they were camping. I need you to show me the person who did it. Would you recognize him?"

I nodded. I remembered the messy, curly hair and the sea-green eyes.

When we got there, they were all gone. There was just a deserted campfire, a pile of ashes in a circle of stones, with beer cans scattered around. I felt sick just being there again, remembering the feeling of panic of the night before.

"Thank you," I said.

"What for?" said Cat's mum.

"For believing me."

"I believe you," she said, "but you're still in a lot of trouble. After all, you let a complete stranger buy you a drink, someone you only met yesterday, who you knew nothing about. You were incredibly naive."

"Are you going to tell my dad?" I asked.

"I'm afraid I have to, Sam," she said. "It would be irresponsible of me not to."

My heart sank. This was not good.

"Who found me?" I asked, remembering the voice that had saved me.

"David."

It was David who saved me. What on earth must he think of me?

I soon found out, when the others came back. David was nowhere to be seen. Niv, Dan and JJ all asked how I was, and then ignored me completely. They knew I was in trouble and they were not going to get involved.

Cat was very upset. She was also angry with me. That was obvious.

"What were you thinking, Sam?" she said. I thought she might burst into tears.

"My drink was spiked," I said. "He put something in my orange juice."

She looked shocked, but also relieved.

"Her drink was *spiked*?" Ryan was suddenly beside us.

"What did he look like? I'll *kill* him!"

He was so angry on my behalf, he looked as if he was capable of murder. Which made me find him, at that moment, surprisingly loveable, for a toadlike brother.

"They've long gone," said Cat's mum.

"You really are stupid," Cat said to me.

"Why are you still mad at me?" I asked. "I made a mistake. I'm sorry if you feel like I've embarrassed you."

"That's not it," said Cat, an edge to her voice. "Ryan told me."

"Told you what?"

"Your mum's not left your dad at all. She's on holiday. I was trying to give you the benefit of the doubt, but now I can see you just don't like being straight with people."

I looked at Cat, who looked accusingly back at me. I wondered when Ryan had told her. I felt terrible.

"They might split up," I protested, not very convincingly.

"I can't *believe* you, Sam," said Cat, and turned her back on me.

On the bus, no one was speaking to me. They were all annoyed that they had to leave early.

My head was throbbing. I felt very queasy, which is not a good way to feel on a minibus. At one point, embarrassingly, I had to ask JJ's dad to stop the bus so I could go outside and be sick.

This had to be a new low point.

"I'd like to get hold of whoever did it," said Ryan, out of the blue. He was obviously still angry, an hour into the bus journey.

"She should have known better," said JJ.

That hurt. Because he was absolutely right. I should have.

"Could you please talk as if I'm actually here?" I said. From being somebody they were considering as a friend, I had been demoted to the position of foolish little girl. Exactly what, with my image change, I'd been trying to avoid. I felt crushed.

When we got home, Ryan, who I knew cared enough to be angry on my behalf, was suddenly silent. Cat's mum had been on the phone to the Emperor of Meat, who was waiting for me, all fired up with indignant rage and ready to give me the telling-off of my life.

"Imagine what your mother would say!" he shouted, waving his arms around emphatically. "It's lucky for you I'm not going to tell her. I should never have let you go to that damned Plastic Spoon Festival. You're grounded for a *month.*"

Then I noticed what he'd done to the house. All the furniture and the floor was covered in dustsheets, and most of the wallpaper was stripped off downstairs. Pots of paint, toolboxes and paint trays and brushes were strewn all around. There was even a sander sitting on the dining room table.

"What are you doing?" I asked. There was no point

arguing about the grounding. I deserved it. In fact, a month was pretty good. I'd expected it to be until I was eighteen.

Dad looked around as if he too was surprised by the scene around us, which was exactly like something out of a DIY show on TV.

"I'm redecorating the house as a surprise for your mum," he said, "and you two are going to help me."

Great, I thought. Not only was I grounded. I was grounded in a bad reality TV DIY show, presented by the Emperor of Meat.

POSITIVES

⊛ I might actually enjoy the experience, playfully dabbing paint on my fellow decorators noses, like they do in the adverts ON TV.

NEGATIVES

⊛ Hours of boring and back-breaking hard work.

⊛ It's never as easy as it looks ON TV.

After lunch, we got started. I wore my horse's head sweatshirt and some old trousers, because I thought it wouldn't matter if I got paint all over them. Not that I got to do any painting. I was given the horrible job of scraping off the ancient woodchip wallpaper and sanding our knackered and dented skirting boards. At least Dad let us listen to local radio rather than his annoying sports chat channel, which made it more bearable.

Ryan was surprisingly eager to help. He seemed like a different person since he'd started trying to impress Cat, like he'd woken up from a long sleep. I mean, suddenly it was possible to actually have a conversation with him. Not that I wanted this when we were decorating, because it usually involved telling me I was scraping the wallpaper off in the wrong way. I mean, how can you scrape it off in the wrong way? Surely it's either off or still on? And what do toads know about decorating anyway?

Gemma rang when we were in full swing. Dad was glaring at me murderously so I had to tell her we couldn't talk for long. Which was annoying, because it's so rare we get to actually speak on the phone.

"Are you OK?" she said. "What happened at the festival?"

"I'm fine, I just can't tell you about it now. We're decorating the house and Dad's not letting me talk to anyone because I'm in trouble. How were your Highland Games?"

"Sam, it was amazing! I've met someone!"

"Wow, that's *fantastic*!"

Dad shouted over, "Get off the phone, Sam. *Right now*."

I could see he was serious.

"Gems, I'm really sorry but I've got to go. I'll try and see if he'll let me talk to you later. I'm really, really pleased for you."

Gemma sounded disappointed. "Oh, OK," she said.

Dad wouldn't let me phone her back later, and he took my laptop *and* phone away! It was so odd, not being able to get in touch with anyone and not being able to see what was going on on Facebook. I hoped that Tania Hamilton wasn't being horrible about me, but there was no way of knowing.

We were working on the house until ten at night when Dad finally said that we'd done enough. My fingers were aching from scraping wallpaper.

"I've taken the week off work," he said, "and I'm calling in a few favours. I reckon we'll have it done for next Saturday. The new kitchen arrives on Tuesday, so we'll need to get the old cupboards out and the tiles off by then."

"We're getting a *new kitchen*?" I was amazed. Mum's wanted a new kitchen for ever.

"I know the type she wants," said Dad. "Then there's the new flooring; it's arriving on Thursday. So we've got to finish the walls downstairs by the end of Wednesday. That could be a late night."

Dad was obviously on a mission. It was as if he was making up for all the years of loafing around with one week of intense, back-breaking activity. Typical of him; it's all or nothing with Dad.

As I lay in bed trying to get to sleep, I wished I could talk to Gemma. I even wondered about sneaking downstairs and calling her, but it was late and I knew she'd get into trouble if her parents heard her phone going off after eleven at night. I couldn't even text her. I wanted to talk to her about everything that had happened.

David had rescued me, and I hadn't had the chance to thank him. I felt sick to think what I must have looked like to him the night before. But then again, I thought, why should it matter?

The truth was, even if he didn't like me the way I wished he did, I wanted him to think well of me. I didn't want him to think I deliberately got myself drunk and copped off with a stranger. I hoped Cat would explain to him what had happened. But that was unlikely. More likely she'd tell him what a liar I was.

Most of all, I was dreading going back to school and facing people like Tania Hamilton. I knew I'd feel so much better if I could talk to Gems.

It took me ages, but I finally managed to fall asleep. I'd just have to deal with tomorrow when it came.

MY STATUS
Sam Wallis
Is grounded and is not allowed on Facebook. Please don't post, I can't reply.
Tania Hamilton Sad case.

Chapter Nineteen

I knew the moment I sat down in history and looked across at David that he was, as I expected, very angry with me. He would not look at me. To him, I was invisible.

I ended up actually concentrating on what Mr Donovan was saying, just to take my mind off it all. Which of course made Mad Eyes Donovan suspicious.

"Sam Wallis!" He approached my desk near the end of the lesson, fixing me with his demented stare. "After weeks of you not concentrating in class, I notice that you are paying particular attention this morning. Can you explain to me why you find thumbscrews so fascinating?"

Of course the whole class found that very funny indeed.

I didn't mind. It feels good to be an expert on something for a change. I could answer any question about thumbscrews and other implements of medieval torture that anyone cares to ask. I hope it comes up in the exams.

When I walked into the lunch hall, Cat was sitting with

Taylor and David and I knew I couldn't join them, so I sat on my own. Darcie and Hanna came in and for a horrible moment I thought they'd join Cat's group, but to my relief they joined me.

"What happened at the festival?" asked Darcie, concerned.

I told them about having my drink spiked, and they were sympathetic.

"It wasn't your fault!" said Hanna. "Why's Cat not talking to you?"

"It's complicated," I said, because I didn't have the heart to explain that I'd lied to Cat, and that I had an embarrassing crush on David, while he preferred my beautiful friend. In short, I was a complete loser.

I felt sick, thinking how much I'd blown everything.

Tania and Angela Murray walked past.

"Look at her *nails*!" said Angela Murray. I glanced down to see that my nails were grubby and torn from scraping wallpaper the night before. I'd been so distracted I'd not even noticed. They did look pretty terrible.

"How'd you do that, Sam?" asked Tania. "Were you round at David Matthieson's house, clawing at his front door to try to get in for a snog? Bad luck it's Cat he likes, not you! You'd better go and get drunk and be sick all over yourself again."

Angela laughed like it was the funniest thing she'd ever heard in her sheeplike life.

"Ignore her," said Darcie.

I was glad when they walked on and I could stop eating. The lasagne tasted like sawdust in my mouth.

I tried to imagine Tania being chased around the athletics track by a herd of goats. Armed with machine guns. It didn't help.

It was in chemistry that I finally got upset. Probably because Darcie was being so nice to me.

"Are you holding up OK?" she said, giving me a sharp look through her protective goggles. We were doing something with acid, or rather Darcie was.

My eyes filled with tears, which I immediately blinked away. I didn't want Darcie to feel embarrassed.

"Listen, I need a favour," I said. "I need to borrow your mobile to phone Gemma. I'll pay you back, I promise."

Darcie handed me her phone without asking any questions. Which is why Darcie Clelland is a hundred per cent solid gold, if you had to pick any element in the periodic table.

I hurried off to the girls' toilets and made the call. Of course I should have realized that Gemma would be in school too, so she would not be able to answer her phone. But at least I could leave a message to try to explain.

"Gems, Sam here. I've borrowed Darcie's mobile, Dad's got mine. I'm not allowed to talk to anybody. Someone spiked my drink at the festival. I'm in a lot of trouble and Tania has got her whole gang turned against me. Cat's not talking to me either because she's found out Mum's not really walked out. I've messed everything up. I really wish

I could talk to you. I'll try to get Dad to let me ring you tonight, though he's still pretty angry at me. Miss you loads."

I think my voice cracked a little when I said "Miss you loads." When I ended the call, I had a little cry. My second bout of crying in the girls' toilets in just a few weeks! This is so unlike me. I mean, my dad's nickname for me is Smiler, for goodness' sake!

I'd never been so happy to hear the school bell go, and rushed home on a magic carpet of relief. The prospect of scraping more wallpaper actually seemed appealing in comparison to having to be in the same building as Tania Hamilton.

Dad worked us hard all evening, again. We were rushing to get the old tiles off in the kitchen and it was tricky. Dad and a mate of his had spent the whole day breaking up the old cabinets and filling a skip, which was in the front drive. He looked absolutely knackered but was determined to get everything ready, so he hardly stopped and we even had to force him to have a cup of tea. I asked if I could ring Gemma but he just glowered at me, which was scary since he was covered in white plaster. He was like Zombie Dad. I decided not to push it.

Ryan was again quite cheerful about helping. He's like a different person since he went to the movies with Cat. Either the story about the girl dying moved him deeply, or he's madly in love. I think I can guess which. Once during the evening, his phone beeped and he read this text and got all pleased with himself. I wondered if it was from Cat, but he's as mysterious as he is smug so I've got no idea.

After a while I got into the whole home makeover thing. There is something deeply satisfying about smashing a tile with a hammer, especially when you're feeling angry about how someone is treating you. Clearing up the rubble with a shovel and a broom is slightly less fun. My already ragged nails looked a lot worse by the end of the evening. The problem was there were no builders' gloves in my size. My hands are not as giant as I'd thought. I had to improvise with a pair of rainbow-coloured fingerless gloves and they just didn't offer enough protection.

At least doing some proper hard work for a change kept me from brooding about things too much. In fact, it made me remember a TV documentary I saw once where children of my age and younger spent their whole days picking up bits of plastic from a rubbish dump to sell so they could buy a loaf of bread. Their lives were unrelenting hard labour and ragged fingernails, and here I was getting upset about Tania Hamilton.

It must have been midnight before we all crawled to bed, but I felt as if I'd done something important and useful, and it was worth it to see Dad's look of satisfaction when the last tile came off.

The next day in English, I didn't turn round because I didn't want to have to see David Matthieson look away from me pointedly. But throughout the whole class I was aware that he was just a couple of rows behind me. I realized that I still liked him so much it actually physically hurt. To have him despise me for my behaviour at the festival was crushing. No wonder he liked Cat; she had so much more self-control and self-respect than I did. I sat, filled with dark thoughts about myself.

We were still doing *Romeo and Juliet*, and so I also had to endure Miss Mooney going on about star-crossed lovers while she crunched Polo mints non-stop.

I'm sure, as she sighed melodramatically and talked about true love, that she was thinking about Mr Ashcroft. Which is why love is totally ridiculous, and why I am ridiculous for liking David Matthieson. Love turns us into prize idiots. After all, it's just, like Sheila said, baboonery.

Tania made some remark about it being a good thing that Juliet wasn't like Sam Wallis, because then she'd be sick all over Romeo. Angela and about half the class fell about laughing.

After English, Taylor told me that I had to sit with him and Cat at lunch. David was obviously back to eating in the library, to make sure he wouldn't have to sit with me.

"You've got to make it up," he said. "I won't have you two falling out."

It was awkward, sitting opposite Cat at lunchtime.

"So how much was actually true about your mum?" she said, getting straight to the point.

"She's been upset at Dad," I said, "and she went off without saying goodbye . . . on this holiday thing."

"Did she really throw a rib-eye steak at him?" asked Taylor.

"No," I admitted, "but I am certain she wanted to. And when you came round for dinner that night, Cat, I thought that she might put a plate of risotto over Dad's head."

"I just don't understand why you had to exaggerate it all." Cat was puzzled.

I hung my head, too embarrassed to even think of taking a bite out of my ham sandwich (I'd given up on pretending to be vegetarian).

"I wanted to seem interesting," I said. "My life's so boring. My dad's a butcher and my mum's a nurse and in the evenings we all watch TV. Your mum's a painter and you're in a *band*. And David's mum is an alternative therapist and they're vegetarian *and* he writes songs!"

Cat shook her head. "You think that's all good? You must be mad! It's not. I *hate* that my dad's not around and I don't have any brothers or sisters. And though I love it that Mum's doing better with her painting, I *hate* it that she forgets to cook half the time and the house is full of dusty old clutter. Being in the band's great, but they act like I'm some little sister they have to protect. I have to keep my guard up *all the time* in case I let them down. It's exhausting!"

I couldn't believe it. I'd had no idea Cat felt that way.

"And another thing!" she said, obviously on a roll. "I know Tania Hamilton is treating you like her worst enemy recently, but she'll get over it and in a couple of weeks she'll leave you alone. But she'll *never* get over hating me, even though I've not done one thing to her except turn up at school this term. People like Tania and Angela always have it in for me. Believe me."

Now I felt really bad. I'd assumed that being Cat must be the best thing in the world, but obviously I was wrong.

MY STATUS
Tania Hamilton
Is not missing Sam on Facebook. Tooooooo sick of hearing about her deeply tragic existence.
Angela Murray Bet even her horse doesn't want to talk to her!
Tania Hamilton LOL. Her horse totally hates her!

Chapter Twenty

After a bearable afternoon – because I didn't bump into Tania or any of her friends – I felt quite hopeful walking home. After Cat had opened up at lunch, I started to think that maybe I could tell her things I'd been holding back. Like just how much I'd liked David and how disappointed I was that he liked her instead of me. Maybe then she'd understand how I was feeling.

When I walked into the house, Dad had the most enormous grin on his face, because the kitchen was fitted and it looked absolutely brilliant. There was a brand new double cooker, gleaming and silver. The worktop was black marble. The cupboards were modern and white, with clever things like sliding drawers to warm your dinner plates. It was top of the range. I couldn't believe it. Dad's friend Ken was busy doing the tiling.

"There's so much still to do," Dad said as I tried to take it all in. "We've got to finish all the downstairs painting before the oak flooring goes down on Thursday. Sam, you're varnishing the new skirting boards. I'll give you a lesson."

Ryan was already at work painting the walls we'd painfully scraped, filled and sanded on the previous nights.

After he finished teaching me how to varnish, Dad started wallpapering a "feature" wall in surprisingly classy wallpaper. There was absolutely no way that Dad could have chosen something like that himself, I decided.

"How did you choose the colour scheme and wallpaper?" I asked him, wondering if he'd hired an interior designer at great expense.

Dad pointed at a pile of magazines on the coffee table. They had various pages marked with Post-it notes with mum's handwriting on them saying things like "lovely colour" and "great sofa".

"Last year your mum went through this phase where she wanted to do up the house. She bought these magazines and went through them . . . marked the things she liked. And I never took a bit of interest."

He looked ashamed, I was glad to see.

When we were having fish and chips later, in the short break Dad allowed us, I decided to risk asking Ryan about him and Cat.

"So, are you actually seeing her then? Officially? She's not told me anything."

He looked at me as if wondering whether he could

211

confide in me. "Yup," he said, and popped another chip into his mouth. He looked incredibly pleased with himself.

"It could be awkward, you know," I said, "with me being friends with her."

Ryan shook his head, looking the happiest I've ever seen him. "I'm OK with it," he said.

"I didn't mean for *you*, you idiot!" I said. "I meant awkward for *me*."

Ryan shrugged. "Not my problem," he said, and he threw his balled-up fish and chip wrapper at the bin, raising his fist in victory when it sailed in.

"He shoots! He *scores*!" he cried.

Although in some respects Ryan has changed, in most he is still my very annoying brother.

When Dad went out to see somebody about a fridge freezer, I knew he would be gone at least fifteen minutes, if not half an hour, and begged Ryan to let me use his laptop to make contact with Gemma. Reluctantly, and perhaps to keep on my good side due to Cat, he agreed. So he's not so annoying, really.

> **Sam Wallis**
> Got Ryan's laptop. Dad doesn't know. I might not have long. Had to talk to you.

> **Gemma Smith**
> Got your phone message. You all right?

Sam Wallis

Better now. Decorating house for Mum coming home this weekend.

Gemma Smith

What's this about having your drink spiked at the festival? Why were you drinking?

Sam Wallis

Found out David likes Cat. I got upset, bumped into fire-eater. He spiked my orange juice. David rescued me. I was sick over people. David not talking to me. Cat only just talking to me again. I'm an idiot.

Gemma Smith

How do you get yourself into those situations? Don't look at Facebook. Tania Hamilton's been being pretty nasty. I've not said anything because I didn't want to give them the satisfaction. I've been so annoyed and upset for you.

Sam Wallis

I thought she'd be doing something like that. I should go and look at Facebook.

Gemma Smith

No. Don't. You'll just get upset.

> **Sam Wallis**
> I need to. Let me look and I'll come back on chat in five minutes.

> **Gemma Smith**
> Sam, don't. I've got stuff to tell you. You said you've not got long.

> **Sam Wallis**
> I've got to see what she's said. Five minutes.

I went on to Facebook and saw the things that Tania had said. I felt sick. I knew she could be nasty but it was gutting to see that she seemed to really hate me. And even worse, to see otherwise OK people like Angela and Becky join in just to impress her. It was so hurtful, I felt like I'd been slapped.

POSITIVES
⊛ NONE ... UNLESS ANY ATTENTION IS BETTER THAN NONE.

NEGATIVES
⊛ HUNDREDS OF PEOPLE WITNESS THE SHAME.
⊛ IT COULD GO VIRAL.
⊛ YOU CAN'T STOP YOURSELF LOOKING TO SEE WHAT ELSE THEY SAY.

✱ It's never good.

I debated about whether to add anything to any of the posts and several times started to but then deleted the words. Gemma was right. Acknowledging it would just please Tania. I decided to defriend her instead. With a few clicks, it was done. Easy.

But by the time I'd debated and been upset and then done that, at least ten minutes had passed, instead of the five I'd promised.

> **Sam Wallis**
> Gems, I've defriended Tania.

> **Gemma Smith** is offline.

Gems had gone, sick of hanging around waiting to chat to me. I didn't blame her. I decided I'd phone her the next night and have a proper chat. Sometimes you just need to speak in person.

The next morning I made a resolution. I was going to apologize to David for my behaviour at the festival, and maybe even tell him the truth about liking him and being disappointed that he liked Cat. Honesty was the best policy, I decided, and then maybe we could all be friends and I could move on from my stupid and hopeless crush on him.

The way Tania was acting, I felt that I needed all the

friends I could get.

So at lunchtime I made my way to the library, where I knew he'd be reading and eating his veggie sandwiches. Maybe I am a pathetically optimistic person, but I was sure everything was going to be all right once I'd sorted it all out.

So I thought.

As soon as I walked into the library I saw Cat sitting with David. They were deep in conversation. I've never seen either of them look so happy. Cat was just sparkling with joy. At one point she reached her hands across the table and David took them, and for about a minute they were looking at each other ecstatically, *while holding hands*!

The way the library is set out, they both had their backs to me. I felt as if someone had reached their hand down my throat, rummaged around in my chest and ripped my heart out. Everything I'd been worried about had come true.

But Cat was *supposed* to be going out with my brother! I thought of Ryan the night before, up a stepladder painting our lounge ceiling and whistling to himself. He was so heartbreakingly happy. And here she was, holding hands in the library with David Matthieson. Looking more radiant than I'd ever seen her.

I couldn't believe how much it hurt, watching them together. I'd convinced myself that I was OK with David preferring Cat. And I was slowly and painfully getting used to the idea. But much, much worse was knowing Cat had lied to me, insisting they were just friends. I felt like the biggest fool ever.

Cat stood up. David stood up. Cat walked round the desk and they hugged.

"See you at eight," said David, which was when I had to get out of the library fast because I could see Cat was about to leave.

I hurried down the corridor, and just after I turned the corner I heard the library door open again behind me.

Cat came into the lunch hall a few minutes later as if nothing had happened. But there was no way I could act as if everything was normal.

"I need some fresh air," I said. I just had to get out of the lunch hall before I did something I might regret. Like sticking my sandwich up Cat's perfectly formed nose.

I felt terrible that evening, seeing Ryan busy decorating, oblivious to what Cat was up to. I decided that before I said anything to him I had to be a hundred per cent sure. David had said something about meeting Cat at eight. I decided to follow him, to see exactly what was going on.

It didn't prove too difficult to slip off at seven thirty, as Dad was now busy upstairs, together with two friends of his who're plasterers, who he promised to pay in Aberdeen Angus beef.

They'd ripped out the tiny built-in dressing table and wardrobe in my bedroom and were plastering my walls ready for them to be painted whatever colour I wanted. This was what I'd been wanting for ages, but I was too upset about Cat to be pleased about it.

I skulked in the front garden till David emerged from his house and started walking towards the town centre. I followed at a safe distance. I wondered what Gems would make of my latest adventure. She'd probably decide I'd lost it, and maybe she'd be right.

David stopped outside the Greenfields Community Centre and looked at his watch. Cat was late. Of course she was, I thought. Someone like Cat would know that she could keep boys waiting.

Then there she was, looking fantastic as usual. They gave each other a huge hug, and then David kissed Cat on the cheek. When they walked into the community centre, he had his arm round her. It could not have been clearer.

I walked home with a heavy heart, wondering how Ryan was going to take it when he found out. I decided not to say anything until I'd confronted Cat. It would be better if she told Ryan herself.

Back home I carried on decorating, too fed up to say much to Ryan, who was in a great mood, poor thing.

"I can't get hold of Cat," he remarked, "her mobile's off. Do you know what she's doing tonight?"

"No," I said, feeling terrible.

The only thing that shook me out of my gloom was a phone call.

"Sam! Turn on your TV!" said a very excited Taylor. "I'm on in the next ad break!"

I pulled the dustsheet off the TV and switched it on just in time for the start of the adverts. Then there was Taylor.

"Puffy-Wheats! Puffy-Wheats! Yummy, scrummy, *tasty* treats!" sang Taylor.

He was dressed as a packet of cereal, with just his arms and legs and his very happy round face sticking out of the giant box. He was dancing madly through a supermarket, waving at shoppers, who were giving him thumbs-up signals and waving in return.

"Is he a friend of yours?" asked Ryan, his paintbrush suspended in amazement.

"Yup," I said, "I'm afraid so."

I was glad I saw Taylor's ad. It made me see that no matter how unlucky you think you are, there's always someone much worse off than you. I may be feeling bad right now, but at least I'm not dancing in a giant cereal packet on television, in front of millions of viewers, being the face of Puffy-Wheats.

MY STATUS
Tania Hamilton
Nice to see Sam back with her loser friends. Where she belongs.
Angela Murray The black nail varnish club, and that's just Taylor!

Chapter Twenty-One

Gemma Smith is offline.

It was ten o'clock. I was upset about Cat and David and their lying. I was sick of varnishing skirting boards, and the fumes from the varnish had given me a headache. I needed to speak to Gemma. Ryan let me borrow his laptop again, but Gems was offline. So I picked up the landline phone and I rang her.

Her mum answered, sounding offhand. Yes, I could speak to Gemma, she would fetch her. Then Gemma came on the phone and told me, quite abruptly, that she was sorry that I sounded upset but that she didn't really want to talk to me.

She said that yesterday I'd not asked once about how she was and about how the Highland Games had gone, even though she'd told me that she'd met someone.

She said that she'd known I didn't have much time but I preferred to check Facebook straight away rather than have a proper conversation. She'd waited for me to look at Facebook and get back to her, but as the minutes ticked on she realized that she was an idiot for thinking that I was a good enough friend to care.

She said that she'd rather not talk to me right now.

She said goodbye.

After she hung up, I sat by the phone, numb. Gemma was right. I was a terrible friend. I'd not cared about her enough to ask about her big news. I'd been too wrapped up in my own problems.

I went to bed soon afterwards, and I lay there thinking about how self-absorbed I'd become lately. I've been so wrapped up in myself I'd forgotten how to be a friend.

I picked up the harmonica, which was beside the bed. My gift from David Matthieson. I put it to my lips, and to suit my mood I should have played a mournful yet beautiful melody. Unfortunately all that came out was a horrible squawking noise. It sounded as if Scuzzball was being tortured.

"*Shut up!*" shouted Ryan from his bedroom.

The next day I forgot that I was avoiding Cat, and walked into the lunch hall. She was sitting with Taylor, who had something of the air of a celebrity about him.

Sure enough, a group of Year 7s nearby were singing:

"Puffy-Wheats! Puffy-Wheats! Yummy, scrummy, *tasty* treats!"

Taylor smiled and waved his hand regally.

"No autographs," I heard him say.

Cat was sitting opposite him, grinning. I just couldn't face joining them. I wanted to confront her, but I didn't feel up to it, not yet. I couldn't go to the library in case David was there, so I ate my lunch wandering the corridors, killing time till afternoon lessons.

Of course I had to run into Tania, Angela and Becky.

"OMG!" said Tania. "She's eating her lunch in the corridor! How sad is that?"

"Give it a rest, Tania," I said, pushing past her. "It was fun at first, but it's getting boring."

"Ooooh! Sorry for pointing out how pathetic your life has become since your bestest friend went away," Tania called after me. "You've been trying to stop acting like a five-year-old, but you *don't know how*! You can't even put on eyeliner properly! And your new friend is just SO good-looking and SO perfect. No wonder everyone likes her! Boo hoo! Poor Sam!"

I didn't reply. As I walked on, I wondered if she had a point. I'd relied completely on Gemma. We'd gone around together being very immature, because it was fun, laughing at everything. Maybe people like Tania had thought we'd been laughing at them. Maybe, sometimes, we had.

What if me and Gems had been as annoying in our own way as Tania and her cronies? That was quite a thought.

It was such a thought, I could think of nothing else all afternoon.

"Who am I?" I kept thinking. "Who am I *really*?" I'd

thought I'd known who I was – goofy Sam. I thought I'd known who I wanted to be – mysterious, interesting, cool Sam. Now it was all mixed up, and neither Sam seemed particularly attractive.

After school, I couldn't bear the idea of going straight home because I'd have to see Ryan, and I hated knowing that he would soon be heartbroken.

So I went around the shops, trying to waste as much time as possible. I was passing a coffee shop when I saw Lucy sitting in the window with her mum. She waved, and so I decided to go in and see her, especially as I'd missed her lesson that Saturday.

"Want to join – us?" asked Lucy, gesturing to an empty chair.

"Yeah, that'd be great," I said, sitting down.

"If it's OK with you, I'll nip over to the post office," said Lucy's mum, obviously pleased that Lucy had a friend to keep her company.

"Want anything?" I asked, standing up.

"I'd love – an ice cream," said Lucy with that expression you get when you are treating yourself to something naughty. "Vanilla, please."

I decided to get myself one too, and soon we were enjoying our ice creams.

"Sheila was very – grumpy – on Saturday," said Lucy. "I asked where you were and she said you were at a festival. She wasn't impressed."

I laughed. "No, and she didn't think much of my eyeliner either."

As soon as I'd said it, I wished I hadn't. I'd forgotten that Lucy didn't like my new look. Now I was asking for more judgement.

But Lucy didn't say anything, just ate some more ice cream and looked at me appraisingly. This made me very self-conscious. OK, so I'd changed my image a little, but not that much, surely?

"Are you coming back?" asked Lucy.

I was surprised. "Of course I am! What made you think I wasn't?"

"Oh – something Sheila said," said Lucy.

"What did she say?"

Lucy shook her head. "I can't – really remember. . . But I think she thinks you're annoyed with her about something."

"Well, she's wrong," I said. "I'll be there on Saturday."

Lucy looked pleased. "I knew you'd never stop coming," she said. "You love Pepper too much to stay away."

"It's not just Pepper," I said. "It's Pepper and *everybody* that I'd miss. I'd even miss Sheila at her grumpiest. I think helping at the stables is the only good thing in my life right now. You know Cat and the boy I like, David? They're seeing each other in secret. I feel stupid and let down and I miss Gemma so much, but she's not talking to me now because I didn't care enough about what was going on with her life."

I sat back, exhausted after blurting it all out like that.

"W-wow!" said Lucy. "Poor you."

"The thing is," I said, "apart from Cat lying to me, I feel like I've brought it all on myself. I feel like I've messed everything up, and without Mum or Gemma to put me right I'm turning into this horrible, selfish person."

Lucy laughed.

"Oh, Sam! You could never be a horrible, selfish person! You're funny and generous and kind, and. . ."

"But I'm *not*!" I interrupted her. "Maybe I've seemed like that to you, but really I'm not. I'm mean and self-centred and envious! Deep down, I'm jealous of Cat for being so beautiful for a start . . . and there was Gemma with big news about her weekend, but I didn't want to know. All I cared about was what people were saying about me on Facebook."

"Listen," said Lucy, "you mustn't be so hard on yourself. Nobody's perfect. Gemma will understand if you explain."

"I hope so," I said, "but here I am going on about myself, and I haven't asked about you. How are you doing?"

Lucy grimaced. "Not so bad," she said. "I think I'm ready for the exams. It's scary though. I want to be a lawyer, a good one. I want to be able to live independently, but who knows? It might not be possible for years."

"I think you'll be brilliant at whatever you do," I said, "especially if you work as hard at it as you have with the horse riding."

"It's good of you to say that," said Lucy. "I need to hear it. But sometimes I don't believe I'll ever be able to get the life I want. I get so frustrated at how much help I need. I want to be able to put the toothpaste on my toothbrush myself. I want to be able to eat without spilling stuff down my front. I'd like to take a bath without it being a major operation. Sometimes, I could just scream."

When she said that, I felt ashamed about how sorry I'd been feeling for myself. We chatted more about her plans.

"Sam," Lucy said later in the conversation, "I meant what I said before. You're great as you are. You shouldn't try to change yourself."

I knew she was talking about my image change and, for the first time, I wondered if she and Sheila might be right. Maybe from being Miss Rainbow I'd gone too far in the other direction. Cat suits that look, but then Cat and I don't look anything like each other. She's dark, I'm blonde. What looks good on her doesn't necessarily look good on me.

When Lucy's mum came back, I said goodbye and headed off home. There was no putting it off any longer. There were lots of improvements to be made, and not just on the house. I needed to do some on myself.

The new floor was down when I got home. It looked great. But while downstairs was beginning to come together, upstairs was still a disaster zone.

Halfway through the evening, I borrowed Ryan's laptop,

took it into my bedroom and looked to see if Gemma was online. She was.

> **Sam Wallis**
> Gems, I'm sorry. Will you talk to me?

There was nothing. No indication of any reply. Two minutes passed. It looked like she didn't want to talk to me, but she didn't go offline. I tried again.

> **Sam Wallis**
> I'm an idiot. The biggest idiot in idiot-land. I am such an idiot, even idiots think I'm an idiot. I am the queen of idiots.

Nothing. Another couple of minutes passed. *I've blown it*, I thought. *I've ruined my friendship, and I deserve Gemma being mad at me.*

Scuzzball padded into my room, eyeing me suspiciously. He was probably looking for signs of me producing his cheerleader's outfit, complete with pom poms, the sight of which would have been his signal to run for his life. I didn't have the heart, even though Scuzzball makes a magnificent cheerleader.

The screen was achingly empty under my last sentence. Nothing. I was waiting for Gems to go offline, dreading it, because then I'd know for sure she never wanted to speak to me again.

...n a little speech bubble appeared by Gemma's name. She was writing something!

> **Gemma Smith**
> Yes, you are an idiot.

> **Sam Wallis**
> I know. I really want to know about what happened at the Highland Games, if you'll tell me.

> **Gemma Smith**
> You don't deserve to know, you are too much of an idiot.

> **Sam Wallis**
> But I'm an extremely nosy idiot.
> Pleeeeeeeeeeeeeeeeeeease!

> **Gemma Smith**
> Oh, all right then. Well . . . I AM IN LOVE! Now I know how you feel about LOYL! His name is Campbell. He has very dark hair and light brown eyes and he is fifteen and scrumptiously yummy! He has muscles on his arms because he works on his dad's farm and he has his OWN FISHING BOAT!

> **Sam Wallis**
> Oh my God he sounds fantastic! More please!

Gemma Smith

His mum loved my knitted scarves, and she got talking to me and my mum. She said what a nice girl I was and that she'd love me to meet her son. I was imagining some awful mummy's boy with his hair parted in the middle, but I said that I'd love to meet him, to be polite. So she disappears and comes back with HIM!!! I could hardly speak!

Sam Wallis

It sounds so old-fashioned!

Gemma Smith

I know!!!!! It is! We arranged that he would take me to the beach barbecue thing, but it was so formal and polite and weird with the mums looking on. It was better once we got away from them and could be on our own. We talked all night, and he wanted to know all about what it's like to live in England. I told him all about you, and Grungefields. I was dying for him to kiss me, but he only gave me a peck on the cheek at the end of the evening and said he'd see me the next day. Then I didn't see him till the afternoon.

Sam Wallis

Oh no! You must have been wondering if he liked you.

Gemma Smith

I was. I mean, it was his mum's idea, not his. For all I knew, he didn't fancy me one bit. Then he appeared out of the crowd and he said he'd been looking for me all day; he'd even gone to my house looking for me. So we spent the rest of the weekend together.

Sam Wallis

And he kissed you?

Gemma Smith

Sam Wallis

He kissed you!

Gemma Smith

!!!!!!!!!!!

Sam Wallis

Have you seen him since the weekend?

Gemma Smith

No, but he is coming to see me next weekend. He's going to take me out on his boat!

Sam Wallis

Ooooooooh!!

Gemma Smith

How are you? I noticed Tania's gone quiet on Facebook. Probably cos you've not replied and she knows you've defriended her. Are things better?

Sam Wallis

Tania's still sniggering at me and being totally stupid. I'm talking to Cat again but she's been lying to me. She's seeing David in secret and she's meant to be going out with Ryan.

Gemma Smith

WHAT?

Sam Wallis

She pretended that they are just friends but it's so obvious it's much more than that. She doesn't know I saw them together, first in the library holding hands and then going out the other night.

Gemma Smith

You've got to talk to her.

Sam Wallis

I'm going to. I just don't know what to say.

Gemma Smith

Tell her she's a two-faced liar!!!!!

Sam Wallis

It's so good to be able to tell you about it. But I'm SO PLEASED FOR YOU! It just shows that even if they take you to the Outer Hebrides, your parents can't stop you!!!! Go girl!!!! I probably should go as we're still decorating.

Gemma Smith

Hee hee. OK. Speak tomorrow? Btw, I've seen the Puffy-Wheats ad!!!!!

Sam Wallis

ROFL. Tomorrow xxxxx

Gemma Smith

xxxxx

It felt so good to chat with Gemma. Suddenly I saw the whole situation through Gemma's and Lucy's eyes.

OK, I'm not perfect. But who is?

Chapter Twenty-Two

MY STATUS
Tania Smith
Saw Sam Wallis in town, with her SPECIAL friend. Two
retards eating ice cream. Too funny.

The phone rang very early in the morning. It was Gemma,
on a bad phone line, telling me about Tania's post on
Facebook. Apparently her post had a picture with it of me
and Lucy in the coffee shop window, eating our ice creams.
I couldn't see it myself as I'd defriended Tania.

"I can't believe it!" I said.

"I'm so angry for Lucy," said Gemma. "I hope she never
sees it, or hears about it."

Ten minutes later the phone rang again. It was Becky
Robinson, sounding upset.

"I hope you know, Sam, that I want nothing to do with
Tania now she's done this."

I'd not realized so many people went online before

they'd even had their breakfast.

The next phone call was from my Aunt Penny in Australia, who insisted on talking to Dad. Gemma must have said something to her. I think Aunt Penny told Dad about all the other nasty comments Tania's made as well. I've never seen him so angry.

"Why didn't you tell me that this girl was bullying you online?" he asked.

I didn't know what to say. Except that it hadn't felt like bullying. Not at first. It happened so gradually, it kind of crept up on me.

During all this I was trying to get ready for school. I was looking for my shoes when the doorbell rang. I opened the door to find David Matthieson standing there.

"Are you OK?" he asked. Somehow, he knew. The news must be spreading fast, I thought.

"I didn't think you were talking to me," I replied, trying to hide the fact that just seeing him there was making me feel shaky.

"Of course I'm talking to you," he said. "So what are you going to do about Tania?"

I shrugged. "Nothing," I said. "I think everyone else has it covered."

I was right.

Dad insisted on driving me and David and Ryan to school in a grim and silent journey, and then he marched off to see the head teacher. A little while later I heard that Tania was collected from school by her mother. She'd been suspended.

A special assembly was called at lunchtime, where we were all lectured about social responsibility and labels and bullying. It was like a nuclear bomb had gone off, the impact was so huge.

Of course loads of people had seen the picture of me and Lucy in the coffee shop window; these things spread like wildfire. I felt removed from the whole thing, suddenly. I felt removed from the nastiness.

What was good, was that nobody even thought of what Tania had said as funny. All morning, people came up to tell me how sorry they were about what she'd done. At lunch, Becky Robinson seemed in shock. Angela Murray was nowhere to be seen.

I was sitting with Cat and Taylor, who spent the whole time talking about how shocked they were and asking if I was OK, and was I *really* OK.

Cat was almost in tears, she was so angry and upset for me and Lucy.

"How could she do it!" she kept saying, outraged.

And I kept thinking: *How could YOU do it, Cat?*

I wanted to talk to Cat, about seeing her with David, but now didn't seem like the right time. Tania's Facebook outrage had made everything else seem unimportant. The person I was really worried about was Lucy. The post had been removed now, but I didn't know if she would have seen it. Greenfields is not a huge town. Lucy is at the upper school. Would anything have reached there? I hoped not. I would have to talk to her.

Chemistry with Darcie felt like an oasis of calm in an otherwise mad day.

"Sorry about what happened," she said, setting out the equipment in a neat row. "I'd like to meet your friend. She's called Lucy, isn't she? She looks like she could be your sister."

I smiled. "She is like a sister really," I said. "You'd like her."

David Matthieson appeared as I was leaving to go home.

"Can I walk with you?" he said.

"OK," I replied, feeling self-conscious. You see, you can't just stop liking someone instantly just because you realize they love somebody else. It takes a while to get over a big crush like the one I had on David Matthieson. And his standing near me was enough to make me feel all hot and bothered and awkward. My face was doing its usual horrible blushing.

"I'm sorry," he said, "for reacting so much to what happened at the festival. I was angry with you for leaving halfway through Mr Bleaney playing and going off with someone you didn't even know. I suppose I thought. . ."

I stopped in my tracks. Was he trying to tell me he cared about what I did? This didn't make sense. I remembered his face as he'd looked at Cat. I'd seen them in the library. I'd seen his arm around her the other night.

I turned to face him, interrupting him. "Listen. I saw you and Cat the other night with your arm round her. And

I saw you in the library holding hands. I know what's going on," I said, "but you have to keep it as this big secret. I thought you were both my friends."

I walked on, quickly enough to give him the message that I wanted nothing to do with him. He was supposed to let me go. But he didn't.

"Sam, stop!" he shouted, hurrying after me. "Please, at least let me explain."

And that's how we ended up in the same coffee shop I'd been in with Lucy. He tried to buy me my hot chocolate, but I insisted on getting my own. I didn't want anything from him. Besides, I still had some of the money from Mum.

I treated myself to the deluxe one with the whipped cream and sprinkles on top. That way, as I heard the truth about him and Cat, at least I'd have something delicious to help ease the pain.

I was not looking forward to this. Still, I had to be fair and hear him out, at least so that I could tell poor Ryan the truth about what was going on.

"We're more than friends," he began, "but not in the way you think. You see, we didn't just know each other from school. We met outside school, unexpectedly."

I nodded, though I was feeling confused. He took a deep breath.

"My dad was a drinker. That's why he left. Mum kicked him out because he promised he'd stop one time too many. Sometimes he got violent; he never hit us or anything, but he'd break things.

"After Dad went, I was sure that somehow it was my fault. I started to get behind at school and miss classes. Mum was really worried, so she found out about this support group for teenagers whose lives have been affected by living with an alcoholic parent. It took me months to get up the nerve to go, but when I went along, guess who was already there?"

"Cat?" I whispered. Of course.

"It was her mum," David explained. "Cat's mum was never as bad as my dad, but she did get to the point where she decided to get some help and stop drinking, so she was getting support, and so was Cat. I hope I'm right in thinking this will go no further."

I nodded. David obviously didn't know that I already knew.

"It was bad in other ways too," he went on. "Cat was being bullied. In school and on Facebook. That's why she's not a member any more. This group of girls had it in for her. I think that's part of the reason she and her mum moved back to Greenfields, not just because of the house. Cat needed a new start. At the time I tried to stand up for her, but the girls just got their boyfriends to try to beat me up, and then I got into even more trouble."

I felt terrible. Cat hadn't told me about the bullying. But then I remembered how she'd said that girls like Tania always hated her. That must have been what she meant.

"Poor Cat," I said, realization dawning. "She must have had an awful time."

"She did," said David. "But she's doing OK now, mostly thanks to finding you again. She really missed you."

"She told you that?"

"Yes. She was always talking about you, this great fun friend called Sam she'd had before, and how she missed you. Do you know, I felt like I knew you before I ever met you?"

"She confided in you a lot," I said.

David nodded. "Yes, you do when you go to a support group. That's why Cat and me are close. But it's not what you think. We're more like brother and sister."

I looked at him, disbelieving. "But I *saw* you. I saw you in the library, holding hands. And then I saw you both at the community centre the other night. You had your arm around her."

I could see David thinking about what had happened in the library. Then he seemed to remember.

"Cat came to the library to tell me that a record company's been in touch. That's why we were holding hands – we couldn't believe it. They like Mr Bleaney. They want to meet the band, and me because I wrote the lyrics of some of the songs. I don't know how it looked to you, but honestly, we were just congratulating each other, that's all. As for the community centre, that's where the support group is. Believe it or not, it's still hard to walk in every month."

Looking back, I saw that what he said was true. In the library, they'd looked ecstatic. I could see why they would have held hands when sharing news like that. As for his arm being round her outside the community centre, I could see it now for what it was, a comforting gesture.

"Can I ask you. . . Did you write the lyrics to 'Looking For You'?"

"Yes," said David, looking puzzled. "Why?"

I could feel my cheeks flush. I looked down.

"I like that song," I said.

"Thanks," His voice sounded pleased, in an embarassed sort of way, but I couldn't look at him. Instead I stirred my drink, watching the sprinkles and cream swirl around and around.

"So you and Cat . . . you're *really* not going out with each other?" I managed to say at last. I sipped my hot chocolate.

"No, I swear. We never have."

I looked up. I could see he was telling the truth, but there was something else I needed to know.

"Did she turn you down?" I asked.

It was hard to believe that David Matthieson could be the only boy in the school immune to Cat.

"Believe it or not, she's not my type," he said.

I couldn't believe it.

"What *is* your type, then?"

He looked at me. "Not Cat. And by the way, you've got a chocolate moustache."

Chapter Twenty-Three

Having got rid of my very alluring chocolate moustache, I walked home with David. What did he mean, I wondered, that his type was "not Cat"? Did this mean he liked hideously ugly girls?

When we arrived outside my house, I wondered if I should ask David in, to show him what we were doing. But before I could say anything he said "Bye" and shot off home. I felt disappointed, but not surprised. After all, I'd just given him a grilling about his friendship with Cat. No wonder he couldn't wait to get away from me.

I wandered into the kitchen to find Dad perched on one of the new stools at the new kitchen counter looking worried.

"What's up?" I asked. "It's looking so good!"

It was looking great. Downstairs was completely finished. A new three-piece suite complemented the pale green walls and stunning feature wall. There was a new sideboard too, and Dad had put the TV on the wall, above the fireplace, which saved loads of space. The brand-new oak floor led through to the kitchen, with new lighting and dining table and chairs, not falling apart like the old ones. It didn't look like our house any more; it looked like something out of a magazine.

"I know," said Dad, "but upstairs is a nightmare, and she's back *tomorrow*! There's three rooms to paint, bathroom flooring to lay and a shower screen to fit. Not to mention putting the fitted wardrobes in – and that's a day's work in itself. Even with you and Ryan helping, I can't do it in time. I've used up all my favours; my mates have all done more than they needed to already. I can't ask them to give up their Friday night as well."

He looked so disappointed.

"We've just got to get some more help," I declared, acting more confident than I felt. "Leave it to me!"

MY STATUS
Sam Wallis
HELP!!!!! This is an SOS to anyone who can hold a paintbrush. We need help to finish decorating our house in time for my mum coming home tomorrow.
Hanna Kermack I'll be along in half an hour.
Becky Robinson Count me in; I'll bring my sisters.
Darcie Clelland I'll be round at six.
Sam Wallis Wear old clothes! Pizza is on us!
Taylor Griffen I'm in. See you soon.

I texted Cat and she said she'd tell David, though I was convinced he wouldn't turn up. I was pretty surprised when he was one of the first to arrive. Dad couldn't believe it when so many people turned up that evening asking what they could do to help.

Taylor arrived in an oversized blue boiler suit with a box of paintbrushes. It was like he was auditioning for a part in a film where he was playing a miniature painter and decorator.

"Even stars should muck in and get their hands dirty now and again," he said, without a hint of irony.

David turned out to be very good at putting together the fitted wardrobes, with the help of Darcie, who actually read the instructions and laid everything out in the right order for him. Dad was able to concentrate on the bathroom flooring and shower panel with Ryan and his friend Matthew's help, while the rest of us painted like our lives depended on it.

I noticed that Taylor and Hanna were getting on particularly well, and wondered if his charm, or celebrity status, had at last worked its magic. Certainly she was howling with laughter at everything he was saying.

By eight o'clock we were getting hungry, so Ryan and Cat went out to get pizzas.

It was while they were out and the rest of us were having a break that the doorbell rang.

I opened it to find Tania Hamilton and Angela Murray on the doorstep.

"I've come to say sorry," said Tania, looking at the ground. I could see how difficult it was for her. She was so like a shadow of her former self, it was quite shocking.

"Come in," I said.

She shook her head. "No, I can't," she said. "I was hoping you'd give me the address of your friend. I need to apologize to her too."

"I tell you what," I said, "come to the stables tomorrow at eleven. She'll be there then. But I've got to warn you, I'm not sure if she's seen it. I don't know if it's a good idea that she even knows about it."

Tania nodded. "I'll see you at eleven," she said. Then she and Angela left.

"Good riddance," said Becky Robinson, when they'd gone.

"She said sorry," I pointed out. "I think she means it. That's enough for me."

Becky shrugged her shoulders. I think she's glad of an excuse to be out of Tania's grip for good.

"Well, I hope you don't mind if I sit with you at lunch from now on," she said.

I smiled. "You're very welcome!"

Cat and Ryan came back with the pizzas, which were lush – probably because we were all starving. Then it was back to the painting. Cat and me were painting my bedroom a fantastic pale purple, which was good because I like purple, and it gave me a chance to talk to her.

I told her what David had told me, about the bullying.

"I hope you don't mind that I know," I said.

"It's OK," she said, not turning round.

I cleared my throat. "We'll have to both be honest with each other from now on," I said. "We should be able to tell each other anything."

Cat stopped painting. Her back was to me, but I could see that she was finding it difficult to find the words for what she wanted to say. At last she spoke.

"The worst of the bullying only lasted a year. Year 7. Dad was travelling a lot with work. Mum felt bad, stuck at home with nobody buying her paintings.

"She thought he was having an affair. She'd been drinking too much for a couple of years, but things suddenly got worse. I used to come home from school and she'd be drunk, and there would be nothing to eat in the house. She got really thin because she never ate. Of course, she'd stopped seeing anyone ages before, including your mum.

"Dad would come home and he'd shout at her for not looking after me, and he'd wash my clothes and stock up the cupboards and fridge, but then he'd go on another trip and it would happen all over again.

"One time I phoned your house, because I wanted to tell you what was happening. I needed a friend. So I dialled the number and it rang, but I hung up before anyone answered."

I walked over and took the paintbrush out of her hand.

"Oh, Cat," I said.

"I did my best to keep everything normal. I ironed my own school shirts and made my own packed lunches. I lied to teachers about why Mum didn't make it to parents' evening or to meetings that the teachers tried to set up with her because they were worried about me, because my marks were slipping. I'd always managed at primary when she wasn't so bad; it was when I went up to Bredborough Secondary I really felt on my own.

"The whole of the first term was all about who fancied who; you know how it is. The other girls would ask me who I liked, but I wasn't interested. I was just trying to keep things together at home. The last thing I needed was being set up with a boyfriend. And I was different to them, because of Mum. I can't quite explain it, but when you have a horrible secret, it's something between you and the rest of the world. It sets you apart. You stop being like everyone else. I'm sure they sensed it.

"Some girls got annoyed because some of the boys they liked best liked me, but I didn't seem to be interested in any of them. Looking back, I should have just gone along with them and agreed that I had a boyfriend. Maybe then I'd have been seen as less of a threat, and maybe they'd have left me alone."

"What did they do?" I asked.

Cat shut her eyes. "They said all sorts of things about me. All not true. It started off as teasing and I ignored it. But it got worse and worse. It turned into a hate campaign. One girl in particular led it. She even turned up at my house one day after school. My mum answered the door and she said, to Mum's face: 'Do you know your daughter's a slut?'

"I think she was hoping from some sort of reaction from my mum, but Mum had already drunk most of a bottle of wine, even though it was only four in the afternoon. I remember hearing Mum say, 'So what if she is?' Mum was slurring her words. It was horrible.

"So of course, this girl went back to school and told everyone that my mum was a drunk. The only good thing was that most people didn't believe her, any more than they believed I was a slut or any of the other lies. You see, nobody cared if things were true or not. What was being said about me wasn't important. It was just that it was being said at all. . ."

Cat couldn't manage any more. I could tell it had been hard enough for her saying what she had already said.

"What you've got to realize," I said, "is that it's not you. It's *never* been you. It's been them. You never deserved what they did."

"The thing is," sniffed Cat, "it's going to happen again. I know it. I've tried so hard. I've joined Mr Bleaney. Everything looks great from the outside. It's like I've had a second chance and I should be happy. But inside I'm *frightened*. I got so used to being kicked when I was down. I suppose I'm waiting for it all to start again."

I sat down beside Cat and put my arm around her.

"You don't need to worry," I said, "believe me. Whatever

happens, I'm going to stick by you, I promise. And so will Darcie and Hanna and Becky and Taylor and David. We're all in this together, and we won't let anyone pick on you again. All right?"

Cat leant against me. "Thanks, Sam," she said.

I reached under the bed and pulled out my keepsake box. I got out the postcard that Cat sent me all those years ago and handed it to her.

"You kept it?" Cat held it, turning it over and looking at it in wonder.

"Of course I did. You were my best friend, remember?" I said.

Cat looked at me. "I hope I can be again," she said. "I know you're close to Gemma. . ."

I squeezed her shoulder. "Now I have *two* best friends. Which is even better than one. But you'd better not forget me when you're famous."

Cat smiled, her eyes still full of tears.

"There's one thing I have to ask you, one more time," I said. "Is it for real, you liking Ryan? I mean, do you *honestly* find him attractive?"

Cat shook her head, laughing. "Can't you see that your brother is actually really cute? He *is*! Loads of girls think so. And he's funny."

So she did like him. Despite his general freakiness.

Maybe, I thought, there is hope for us all. Maybe beauty really *is* in the eye of the beholder, and not in the fashion pages of the magazines.

MY STATUS
Sam Wallis
Wants to thank everyone who helped tonight.
Taylor Griffen No worries.
Gemma Smith Well done all of you! Can't wait to hear what your mum thinks.
Penny Griffiths Photos, please!

Chapter Twenty-Four

We were painting till almost midnight, but we got it finished. Once everyone had left, me and Dad and Ryan were up till two in the morning, cleaning up and arranging furniture so that everything was perfect. I fell into bed exhausted but satisfied. I wished it was Saturday afternoon already, so that I could see Mum's reaction.

In the morning, I made sure I got to the stables early so that I could talk to Sheila about Tania turning up to see Lucy.

"What a silly girl," said Sheila. "I hope Lucy's OK."

We soon found out that Lucy was absolutely fine. She'd not actually seen the post, but a friend had.

"I'm – just glad they took it down so quickly," said Lucy. "My mum would get more upset than I was. I'm used to it."

"You're *used* to it?" I said in amazement.

"Yes. People have said things like that to me on the street, or things like it. I think they're sometimes mean because seeing me in my wheelchair makes them uncomfortable, so that's how they react. They're just frightened, really.

"It's so frustrating, that people don't see past my disability. Even people who want to be nice assume I'm somehow incapable of understanding them just because I'm in a wheelchair. They'll talk to my mum instead and say things like "does she like the sunshine, then?" It's so patronizing, I could scream. I don't think you've any idea what people can be like."

I shook my head. "Well, if they can be like that, I'm *disgusted*," I said. "I mean, any single one of us could end up in a wheelchair for any number of reasons, including old age. I just don't get it."

A car arrived. It was Tania, with her mum and dad.

"I want to hear you apologize," Tania's dad said to her, and you could see he was incredibly angry.

"I'm so sorry," Tania whispered. She really did look devastated.

"I – think," said Lucy, looking at Tania with an understanding and compassion that she did not deserve, "you really are."

With Tania coming round, I'd not had time to do all my jobs before the lessons, so I agreed with Sheila I'd come back later to finish off. I rushed home, hoping I'd be there for Mum arriving.

When I got in, Dad was pacing up and down. He was wearing his smartest clothes, as if he was going to a party or out on a date. Ryan was polishing the kitchen work surface until it gleamed. I wanted to pinch myself. What had happened to my father and brother in the past few weeks?

I did a quick tour of the house to make sure that everything was just right. Every single room was transformed. The best room of all was Mum and Dad's bedroom. Apart from the fitted wardrobes, there was a new bed, with luxurious new bedding, a silk canopy and a beautiful sheepskin rug on the floor. Dad had even bought an armchair for the bedroom, because he'd remembered that Mum had always said she'd like one. My room looked great too, with its purple walls and more grown-up wardrobe and chest of drawers, and even a new desk.

"Dad," I asked when I got back downstairs, "how did you afford all of this?"

Dad winked at me. "I'm the Emperor of Meat!" he said. "So of course I had a bit put away for a rainy day. I've always wanted a sports car, something flashy." He looked wistful.

"Middle-aged men in sports cars look sad," I said. "I think you've made the right decision."

"There's enough left over to take your mum to Venice," Dad added, "but don't tell her. I'm going to give her the tickets tonight."

It was so sweet, seeing my dad acting this way. Perhaps absence really does make the heart grow fonder. Certainly there's no way Dad's going to take Mum for granted again.

Ryan called out, "The taxi's here!"

We looked out of the window, and saw Nosy Norah and Mum getting out of a taxi. Mum looked slimmer, tanned, and more relaxed than I've seen her in years.

"Doesn't she look beautiful? Can you see it now?" I said to Dad.

Dad turned and looked at me as if I'd said something completely idiotic.

"Of course she does," he said. "Your mum's *always* been beautiful."

Then I realized something immense.

Dad hadn't ever thought that Mum *wasn't* beautiful! Perhaps he stopped noticing a new haircut or a different dress here or there, but it wasn't because he didn't care. It was because he already thought she was the most beautiful woman in the world, inside and out. Which is what love is all about, I suppose.

I heard the front door bang and had to smile as I watched Dad flying down the front path to grab her in a huge bear hug.

They hugged for slightly too long, I have to say. Certainly Norah looked embarrassed, and said a hurried goodbye, scuttling off to her own house.

Then Dad brought Mum up to the front door and opened it with a flourish. The expression on her face when she saw the living room from the hallway was something to behold. Complete shock, then disbelief, and then delight.

"Sam!" she cried when she saw me.

It felt good, hugging her. I'd not realized how much I'd missed her. I'd never been apart from her for so long, and I'd not realized what an anchor she is for me, keeping me grounded. It was good to have her home again. Even Ryan moved forward and gave her a hug, which probably shocked her more than the newly decorated room.

"I can't believe you've decorated it in just a few weeks!" she was saying. "It's beautiful. You picked out everything that I liked in those magazines!"

"Here's another surprise for you," said Dad, leading her into the kitchen, where she promptly burst into floods of tears.

"We've done the *whole house!*" I cried, practically jumping up and down with excitement.

Mum was still sobbing. She was overwhelmed. Dad had to get her a glass of water.

"But . . . how did you manage it?" she kept asking, as we led her from room to room.

"Don't worry about how we did it," said Dad. "Just enjoy it!"

Back in the kitchen, Mum sat at the new dining table, her eyes still red from all the crying, and smiled. She was smiling partly because she was so pleased about the house, and partly because Dad was making her a cup of tea.

"You've turned our home into a *palace*," she said. "This is the best present anyone's ever given me!"

I smiled. Dad had come up trumps. As far as anniversary

presents go, this was certainly a step or two up from the rib-eye steak.

Later on, I cycled back to the stables, to finish off my work. I felt exhausted after my late night the night before and all the excitement of Mum coming home, but I couldn't let Sheila down.

I was on the last stable, totally mucky and covered in straw, when the tiredness almost overcame me. I had to stop, and I leant on my rake for a minute with my eyes closed, wishing I could nod off.

"No sleeping on the job!" said a voice. I opened my eyes. It was David Matthieson. In my stable!

"What are you doing here?" I asked, wondering if I was actually asleep leaning on the rake and this was a weird dream.

"It's great you're so pleased to see me," he said, and then I knew I wasn't dreaming.

I looked down and remembered I was wearing the horse's head sweatshirt. This was great. Here I was covered in manure, wearing the paint-splattered horse's head sweatshirt, with my hair sticking up and full of straw, and my face a bright red, shiny beacon. I was the old, scruffy Sam at her absolute worst.

Maybe he'd come by to get his sister, I thought. I wished he'd go away and stop staring at me. I felt far too tired to humiliate myself any more.

"I need to talk to you," he said.

"Really?"

"Yeah. I wanted to last night, but there wasn't the right moment, what with everybody around."

"Oh." I didn't know what to say. What did he want to talk to me about?

"I know you're not vegetarian," he said. "I mean, I've always known your dad's a butcher."

I wished the ground would swallow me up. This was awful. He'd come to tell me what a fraud I was.

"I think it happened at the farmers' market," he continued. "That's when I realized I really liked you."

"You *like* me?" I managed.

"You were so funny," he continued, "Your Positives and Negatives list just cracked me up."

"I'm glad I'm so . . . entertaining," I said. "But I don't understand. What do you mean?"

I wondered if my tiredness was making me so fuzzy-headed I couldn't think clearly.

"I like you, but not just as a friend," said David patiently.

"*Not just as a friend?*" I repeated, not believing what he was saying. I really was beginning to sound like a very dense parrot. I couldn't believe what he was saying. I'd lost all hope when I saw his face when he was watching Cat sing at the festival.

Of course now I knew why he'd been so moved. It had dawned on me in the coffee shop. It wasn't because he liked her. It was because she'd been singing *his song*.

He'd been telling the truth. Cat really wasn't his type. I was.

I looked at him, realization dawning at last. He stepped forward and took the rake from me, leaning it on the wall.

"You're sweet, you're funny, and you're just about the nicest person I've ever met," he said. "I've liked you ever since I met you. In fact, I think I liked you *before* I met you. Now, do I have a chance? Or have I messed things up completely?"

This was unbelievable. There I was standing covered in manure, in a horse's head sweatshirt, with straw in my hair. And David Matthieson was asking me if *he* had a chance.

"Yes," I said, "there's a chance. Actually, there's *more* than a chance."

And then, of course, he kissed me.

POSITIVES

* TOO MANY to list.

NEGATIVES

* NONE.

Things have been pretty good ever since.

Tania has changed for the better, at least for the moment. She and Angela don't walk about like they own the lunch hall any more. She's even been making an effort to be nice to me and Cat, which is slightly unnerving.

Cat and Ryan are still going to lame films. Strangely, I don't mind too much. The other week, she got him to take her to a sing-along *Mamma Mia*. Which means he *must* be in love.

I tried to teach myself the harmonica, but I turned out to be as bad at it as I am at singing and everything else musical. I'll just have to settle for being a groupie.

Mr Bleaney's been signed by a small but very cool record label, who have big plans for them, and for David.

Miss Mooney is now Mrs Ashcroft, but she's still Looney Mooney to us.

Taylor's been so successful as the new face of Puffy-Wheats, they've signed him up for five more adverts. In one, he has to waterski. I can't wait.

Scuzzball has a new biker's outfit. He loves it really. (I think.) And I've bought some new ironic T-shirts and some other clothes that aren't black and purple. Why change a winning formula?

Mum and Dad are off soon for their second honeymoon. And do you know what Mum says she appreciates most of all? Not the new kitchen or Venice . . . but Dad making her cups of tea! Really, he could have saved himself a fortune.

Gemma and Campbell are continuing their Highland fling. I just hope they're not scaring off all the seals. Her parents have decided to stay there even after they've finished their research stuff but Gemma seems OK about it. Dad's putting Skype on my laptop so we can chat properly. She'll always be my best friend but I know how to be without her now.

And that is just to be myself, which is a massive and enormous relief. Especially as David Matthieson (or LOML) seems, for some inexplicable reason, to like me this way.

Being yourself is *so much easier*. In fact, I'd highly recommend it.

Look out for more from
Jenny Smith

Diary of a
PARENT
TRAINER

Danger of
overheating
and explosion!

Take
control of
your Grown-Up!

Easily
breakable.
Handle
with care.

Bank of
Mum

Do not let small
children operate
your Grown-Up.

Jenny Smith

Is your parent COMPLETELY OUT OF CONTROL?

YOU NEED THIS BOOK!

Katie Sutton is a parent trainer extraordinaire, and also, quite possibly, an undiscovered genius.

Read her diary, it could CHANGE YOUR LIFE! Or it might not... Still, it's worth a try.

"An enjoyable, feel-good read!"
Chris Higgins

CONGRATULATIONS!

You are in possession of at least one Grown-Up. You have probably had your Grown-Up for some time, possibly all of your life. Now, at last, you can discover the skills you need to operate them successfully.

This easy-to-follow User's Guide will help you to:
* achieve optimum performance from your Grown-Up or Grown-Ups
* undertake straightforward maintenance and repairs
* ensure smooth operation, in most situations.

CAUTION

Your Grown-Up incorporates many complex modes and functions. Familiarization with these is ESSENTIAL before difficult manoeuvres are attempted.

BEFORE USING YOUR GROWN-UP

Read this guide. It contains detailed information on the operation and care of your Grown-Up. Keep it safe and easy to access for future reference.

Tuesday 28th July 4.23 p.m.

In case you're wondering what undiscovered genius is writing this User's Guide, it's me!

My name's Katie Sutton, I'm thirteen years old and I may, quite possibly, be one of the world's leading experts in Grown-Up behaviour. For many years I've been studying their strange modes and functions – both in the wild and in captivity.

I like to think of myself as a bit like the famous wildlife expert David Attenborough – only instead of studying chimps, hyenas and fruit bats, I'm studying my mum, my nan and my Auntie Julie.

My studies of them, and of other Grown-Ups I've encountered, have led me to write this excellent guide. After all, someone needs to . . . and who better than an expert on Grown-Up behaviour like myself? You see, it's a jungle out there. One that's *full* of Grown-Ups. And according to the law of the jungle, you either eat or you get eaten. . .

In this comprehensive guide, I'm going to share with you my secret knowledge of Grown-Ups, gained from years of intensive study and experimentation.

You too can become highly skilled at:
1) understanding their insane behaviour
2) predicting their next moves
3) operating them to your best advantage.

With my help, I guarantee you can stay one step ahead of your Grown-Ups so you can survive their embarrassing weirdnesses. How cool is that?